More Praise fo

Sing to It

"[Amy Hempel is] an essential voice in contemporary American short fiction. . . . [*Sing to It*] offers Hempel at her best: oscillating between hilarity and pain in a way that feels utterly human."

—*Time*

"Scintillating as the blade of a knife . . . The verisimilar quality of this storytelling is powerful. Ms. Hempel's stories compel us to rereading in much the same way we review (or reread) interactions in everyday life, attempting to piece together what really happened, what was actually being said. . . . When there is a shock, a crisis, a scene of horror, Ms. Hempel sings to it, and the result is an exquisite collection by a master of the genre."

—*The Wall Street Journal*

"It's astonishing that Hempel can pack so much emotion into so few words. . . . There's not a story in *Sing to It* that's less than brilliant, and the collection itself is even greater than the sum of its parts. Hempel occasionally draws comparisons to authors like Mary Robison and Joy Williams, but she writes like nobody else—she's an irreplaceable literary treasure who has mastered the art of the short story more skillfully than just about any other writer out there. *Sing to It* is a quiet masterpiece by a true American original."

—NPR Books

"Gorgeously distilled, archly witty, and daringly empathetic tales . . . Hempel is a master miniaturist, capturing in exquisitely nuanced sentences the sensuous, cerebral, and spiritual cascade of existence, homing in on pain and humor and the wisdom each can engender."

—*Booklist*

"Short story virtuoso Hempel's first collection since 2006 consists of fifteen characteristically bold, disconcerting, knockout stories that highlight her signature style with its condensed prose, quirky narrators, and touching, disturbing, transcendent moments."

—*Publishers Weekly* (starred review)

"A dizzying array of short fiction . . . Hempel packs a lot into her narrow spaces: nuance, longing, love, and loss. The brilliance of the writing resides in the way Hempel manages to tell us everything in spite of her narrator's reticence, teaching us to read between the lines."

—*Kirkus Reviews* (starred review)

"Each purified sentence [in *Sing to It*] is itself a story, a kind of suspended enigma. . . . Hempel, like some practical genius of the forest, can make living structures out of what look like mere bric-a-brac, leavings, residue. It's astonishing how little she needs to get something up and going on the page. A pun, a malapropism, or a ghost rhyme is spark enough."

—James Wood, *The New Yorker*

"Hempel packs a great deal into the briefest of fictions, creating balanced and nuanced stories of longing, love, and loss."

—*BookPage*

"Attention short story fans: Amy Hempel is back with her first collection of short stories in over a decade. Some are just a page long and others are like small novellas, but they're all astonishingly rhythmic and textured."

—*HelloGiggles*

"Turning the pages [in *Sing to It*] is like swimming in a lake and suddenly finding the bottom drop out beneath you, leaving you to get your bearings amid unanticipated depths."

—Ruth Franklin, *The Atlantic*

"[Hempel's] stories . . . burrow inside you, dogging your thoughts for days. . . . Hempel has both a better feel for the vicissitudes of the world and a better imagination than you do."

—Cory Oldweiler, *amNY*

Also by Amy Hempel

Reasons to Live

At the Gates of the Animal Kingdom

Tumble Home

The Dog of the Marriage

The Collected Stories

With Jill Ciment, as A.J. Rich

The Hand That Feeds You

Sing to It

Stories

Amy Hempel

Scribner

New York London Toronto Sydney New Delhi

Scribner
An Imprint of Simon & Schuster, Inc.
1230 Avenue of the Americas
New York, NY 10020

Copyright © 2019 by Amy Hempel

First Scribner trade paperback edition November 2019

SCRIBNER and design are registered trademarks of The Gale Group, Inc.,
used under license by Simon & Schuster, Inc., the publisher of this work.

For information about special discounts for bulk purchases,
please contact Simon & Schuster Special Sales at 1-866-506-1949 or
business@simonandschuster.com.

The Simon & Schuster Speakers Bureau can bring authors to
your live event. For more information or to book an event, contact the
Simon & Schuster Speakers Bureau at 1-866-248-3049
or visit our website at www.simonspeakers.com.

Interior design by Kyle Kabel

Manufactured in the United States of America

1   3   5   7   9   10   8   6   4   2

Library of Congress Cataloging-in-Publication Data

Names: Hempel, Amy, author. Title: Sing to it / Amy Hempel.
Description: First Scribner hardcover edition. | New York : Scribner, 2019. |
Includes bibliographical references.
Identifiers: LCCN 2018045523| ISBN 9781982109110 (hardcover) |
ISBN 9781982109127 (pbk.) | ISBN 9781982109134 (ebook)
Classification: LCC PS3558.E47916 A6 2019 | DDC 813/.54—dc23
LC record available at https://lccn.loc.gov/2018045523

ISBN 978-1-9821-0911-0
ISBN 978-1-9821-0912-7 (pbk)
ISBN 978-1-9821-0913-4 (ebook)

To Gloria Vanderbilt Cooper

Contents

Sing to It

*A*t the end, he said, No metaphors! Nothing is like anything else. Except he said to me before he said that, Make your hands a hammock for me. So there was one.

He said, Not even the rain—he quoted the poet—not even the rain has such small hands. So there was another.

At the end, I wanted to comfort him. But what I said was, Sing to it. The Arab proverb: When danger approaches, sing to it.

Except I said to him before I said that, No metaphors! No one is like anyone else. And he said, Please.

So—at the end, I made my hands a hammock for him.

My arms the trees.

The Orphan Lamb

*H*e carved the coat off the dead winter lamb, wiped her blood on his pants to keep a grip, circling first the hooves and cutting straight up each leg, then punching the skin loose from muscle and bone.

He tied the skin with twine over the body of the orphan lamb so the grieving ewe would know the scent and let the orphan lamb nurse.

Or so he said.

This was seduction. This was the story he told, of all the farm boy stories he might have told. He chose the one where brutality saves a life. He wanted me to feel, when he fitted his body over mine, that this was how I would go on, this was how I would be known.

A Full-Service Shelter

They knew me as one who shot reeking crap out of
cages with a hose.

—Leonard Michaels, "In the Fifties"

They knew me as one who shot reeking crap out of cages
with a hose—and liked it. And would rather do that
than go to a movie or have dinner with a friend. They knew
me as one who came two nights a week, who came at four and
stayed till after ten, and knew it was not enough, because
there was no such thing as enough at the animal shelter in
Spanish Harlem that was run by the city, which kept cutting
the funds.

They knew us as the ones who checked the day's euth list
for the names of the dogs scheduled to be killed the next
morning, who came to take the death-row dogs, who were
mostly pit bulls, for a last long walk, brought them good
dinners, cleaned out their kennels, and made their beds
with beach towels and bath mats and Scooby-Doo fleece
blankets still warm from industrial dryers. They knew me
as one who made their beds less neatly over the course of
a difficult evening, who thought of the artist whose young

11

daughter came to visit his studio, pointed to the painting she liked, and asked, "Why didn't you make them *all* good?"

They knew us as the ones who put pigs' ears on their pillows, like chocolates in a good hotel. They knew us as vocal vegetarians who brought them cooked meat—roast turkey, rare roast beef, and honey-glazed ham—to top off the canned food we supplied, which was still better than what they were fed there. They knew us as the ones who fed them when they were awake, instead of waking them at 2:00 A.M. for feeding, the way the overnight staff had been ordered by a director who felt they did not have enough to do.

They knew me as one who spoke no Spanish, who could say only "Sí, sí" when someone said about a dog I was walking, "Que lindo!" And when a thuggish guy approached too fast, then said, "That's a handsome dude," look how we exploded another stereotype in a neighborhood recovering from itself.

They knew us as the ones who had no time for the argument that caring about animals means you don't also care about people; one of us did! Evelyne, a pediatrician who treated abused children.

They knew us as the ones who got tetanus shots and rabies shots—the latter still a series but no longer in the stomach—and who closed the bites and gashes on our arms with Krazy Glue—not the medical grade, but the kind you find at hardware stores, instead of going for stitches to the ER, where we would have had to report the dog, who would then be put to death.

They knew us as the ones who argued the names assigned at intake, saying, "Who will adopt a dog named Nixon?" And when Nixon's name was changed—changed to Dahmer—we ragged on them again, then just let it go when the final name assigned was O.G., Original Gangster. There was always a "Baby" on one of the wards so that staff could write on the kennel card, "No one puts Baby in the corner," and they finally stopped using "Precious" after a senior kennel worker said of a noble, aged rottie, "I fucking hate this name, but this is a good dog." (Though often they got it right; they named the cowboy-colored pocket pit who thought he was a big stud Man Man.)

They knew me as one who did not bother wearing latex gloves or gauzy scrubs to handle the dogs in the sick ward, who wore gloves only when a dog had swallowed his rabies tag, and I had to feel for it in feces. They knew me as one who gave a pit bull a rawhide chew stick swirled in peanut butter, then, after he spit it up and wanted it back, cleaned it off and gave it to him so he could have . . . closure.

They knew us as the ones who put our fingers in mouths to retrieve a watch, a cell phone, a red bicycle reflector that a dog sucked on like a lozenge. They knew me as one who shot reeking crap out of cages with a hose, who scoured metal walls and perforated metal floors with Trifectant, the syrupy, yellow chemical wash that foamed into the mess, and then towel-dried the kennel and liked the tangible improvement— like mowing a lawn or ironing a shirt—that reduced their anxiety by even that much.

They knew me as one who, early on, went to tell a vet tech the good news that three dogs had been rescued from that morning's list of twelve, to which the tech said, "*That* blows—I already filled twelve syringes."

They knew us as the ones who repeatedly thanked the other vet tech, the one who was reprimanded for refusing to kill Charlie, the pit bull adopted less than twenty-four hours later by a family who sent us photos of their five-year-old daughter asleep atop Charlie, the whole story like a children's book, or maybe a *German* children's book. And we kept thanking the vet tech, until he was fired for killing two of the wrong dogs, their six-digit ID numbers one digit off. He didn't catch the mistake, but neither had the kennel worker who brought him the wrong dogs, and who still had his job.

They knew us as those who found them magnificent with their wide-spaced eyes and powerfully muscled bodies, their sense of humor and spirit, the way they were "first to the dance and last to leave," even in a House of Horrors, the way stillness would take them over as they pushed their heads into our stomachs while sitting in our laps. They knew us as those whose enthusiasm for them was palpable, Rebecca falling in love with them "at first sight, second sight, third sight," and Yolanda tending to them with broken fingers still in a cast, and Joy and the rest with their surpassing competence and compassion. They knew us as those who would sometimes need to take out a Chihuahua—"like walking an ant," Laurie said—for a break. They knew us as those who didn't mind when they backwashed our coffee, when they licked the paper cup the moment we looked away. They knew us as the ones who worked for free, who felt that an hour stroking a blanket-wrapped dog whose head never left your lap and who was killed the next morning was time well spent.

They knew me as the least knowledgeable one there, whose mistakes were witnessed by those who knew better.

They knew me as one who liked to apply the phrase "the ideal version of"—as in "Cure Chanel's mange and you'll see the ideal version of herself"—but did not like the term "comfort zone," and thought one should try to move beyond it.

They knew me as one who was unsure of small dogs, having grown up with large breeds and knowing how to read them, but still afraid of the Presa Canarios, the molossers bred in the Canary Islands, with their dark bulk and bloodshot bedroom eyes, since I had lived in San Francisco when a pair of them loose in a tony apartment house had killed a friend of mine who had stopped to check her mail and could not get her door unlocked before the attack began.

They knew me as one who called one of their number a dick when he knocked me over and I slammed into a steel bolt that left me bleeding from just above an eye. They knew me as one who guided them to step over the thick coiled hose in the packed garage that was being used weekly by a member of the board of directors to wash his car the city paid for. He never went inside the building.

They knew us as the ones who attached a life-size plastic horse's head to a tree in the fenced-in junkyard backyard, where the dogs could be taken to run off leash one at a time, and to sniff the horse's head before lifting a leg against it. They knew us as those who circulated photos of two pit littermates dive-bombing each other under the blankets of a bed to get closer to the largehearted woman who had adopted them both.

They knew us as the ones who took them out, those rated "no concern" and "mild," also "moderate," and even "severe," though never the red-stamped "caution" dogs. Although some of the sweetest dogs were the ones rated "moderate," which was puzzling until we realized that behavior testing was done when a stray was brought in by police or a dog surrendered by his owner, when they were most scared. "Fearful" is the new "moderate." And how do you think a starving dog will score on "resources guarding" when you try to take away a bowl of food! They knew me as one who never handled the "questionable" dogs, because that meant they could turn on you in an instant, you wouldn't know what was coming, and some of us got enough of that outside the shelter.

They knew me as one whom Enrique had it in for, the kennel worker who had asked me to take out a 150-pound Cane Corso, and when I said, "Isn't he 'severe'?" said, "Naw, he's a good boy," and when I looked up his card he was not only "severe," he was also DOH-HB hold—Department of Health hold for Human Bite. He had bitten his owner.

They knew me as one who forgave Enrique when he slipped on the newly installed floor while subduing a frightened mastiff, fell, and punctured a lung. After voting to spend nearly fifty thousand dollars to replace the facility's floor, the board then had to allocate funds to bring in a crew with sanders to rough up the pricey new floor. The allocated funds were diverted from Supplies, so kennel staff had to ask us, the volunteers, for food when they ran out because feeding the dogs had not factored into the board's decision.

They knew me as one who held the scarred muzzle of a long-nosed mutt in sick ward and sang "There is a nose in Spanish Harlem" until he slept.

They knew me as one who refused to lock the padlocks on their kennels, the locks a new requirement after someone stole a puppy from Small Dog Adoptions, and which guarantee the dogs will die in the event the place catches fire.

They knew me as one who asked them stupid questions— "How did you get so cute?"—and answered the questions stupidly, saying on behalf of the giddy dog, "I was born cute and kept getting cuter." They knew me as one who talked baby talk to the babies, and spoke in a normal voice about current events to those who enjoyed this sort of discourse during their one-on-ones. I told an elderly pittie about the World War II hero who died in his nineties this year in a Florida hospital after having been subdued while in emotional distress by the use of a metal cage that was fixed in place over his bed. The Posey cage had been outlawed in Eastern Europe, yet was still somehow available in Florida. Caged in the space of his bed, "he died like a dog," people said.

They knew us as the ones who wrote Congress in support of laws made necessary by human cruelty and named for canine victims: Oreo's Law, Nitro's Law, the law for the hero dog from Afghanistan, and that's just this year.

They knew me as one who loved in them what I recoiled

from in people: the patent need, the clinging, the appetite. They knew me as one who saw their souls in their faces, who had never seen eyes more expressive than theirs in colors of clover honey, root beer, riverbed, and the tricolor "cracked-glass" eyes of a Catahoula, rare to find up north. They knew us as the ones who wrote their biographies to post to rescue groups, campaigning for the rescue of dogs that we likened to Cleopatra, the Lone Ranger, or Charlie Chaplin's little tramp, to John Wayne, Johnny Depp, and, of course, Brad Pitt, asking each other if we'd gone overboard or gone soft, like Lennie in *Of Mice and Men*. They knew us as the ones who tried to gauge what they had been through, as when Laurie said of a dog with shunts draining wounds on his head, "He looks exhausted even when he's asleep."

They knew us as the ones who wrote letters to the mayor pointing out that the Department of Health had vastly underestimated the number of dogs in the city to clear itself of misconduct for failing to license more. The political term for this is "inflating their compliance record." They knew Joy as the stellar investigator who told the rest of us that the governor helped boost the state budget by helping himself to funds that had been set aside to subsidize spay-neuter services throughout the state.

They knew that? They seemed to know that, just as they seemed to appreciate Joy's attempt to make a new worker understand that staff had not "forgotten" to write down the times they had walked certain dogs, that the blank space under dates on the log sheets three days in a row meant that those dogs had not been walked in three days. "When the budget was cut by a million and a half," Joy began. But the new worker did not believe her.

They knew us as the ones who decoded reasons for surrender and knew that "don't have time" for an elderly, ill dog meant the owner had been hit hard by the ruined economy and could not afford veterinary bills. They knew us as the ones who doted on "throwaway moms," lactating dogs left tied to posts in the Bronx after the owners sold their puppies, and the terrified young bait dogs—we would do anything for them—their heads and bodies crossed with scars like unlucky life lines in a human hand, yet whose tails still wagged when we reached to pet them. They knew me as one who changed her mind about Presa Canarios when I found one wearing an e-collar that kept him from reaching his food. I had to hold his bowl up to his mouth inside the plastic cone for him to eat; I lost my fear of Presas.

They knew me as one who had Bully Project on speed dial, who knew that owning more than five dogs in Connecticut was, legally, hoarding, who regularly "fake-pulled" a much-loved dog when I found that dog on the list, pretending to be a rescue group, so that in the twenty-four hours it took for the shelter manager to learn it was fake, the dog would have time to be pulled for real.

They knew me as one who got jacked up on rage and didn't know what to do with it, until a dog dug a ball from a corner of his kennel and brought it to my side, as though to ask, "Have you thought of this?"

They knew me as one who learned a phrase of Spanish—"Lo siento mucho," I am so sorry—and used it often in the lobby when handed a dog by owners who faced eviction by the New York City Housing Authority if they didn't surrender their pit.

They knew me as one who wrote a plea for a dog named Storm, due to be killed the next morning, and posted the plea and then went home, to learn the next day that there had been two dogs named Storm in the shelter that night, and the one who needed the plea had been killed that morning—I had failed to check the ID number of the dog. So this is not about heroics; it's about an impossible job. I joined them in filth and fear, and then I left them there.

They knew me as one who walked them past the homeless man on East 110th who said, "You want to rescue somebody, rescue *me*."

They knew me as one who saw through the windowed panel in a closed ward door a dog lift first one front paw and then the other, offering a paw to shake though there was no one there, doing a trick he had once been taught and praised for, a dog not yet damaged but desperate.

They knew me as one who decoded the civic boast of a "full-service" shelter, that it means the place kills animals, that the "full service" offered is death.

They knew me as one who learned that the funds allocated for the dangerous new floor had also been taken from Medical, that the board had determined as "nonessential" the first injection, the sedative before the injection of pentobarbital that kills them, and since it will take up to fifteen seconds for the pentobarb to work, the dogs are then made to walk across the room to join the stack of bodies, only some of which are bagged. This will be the dogs' last image of life on earth. My fantasy has them waking to find themselves paddling with full stomachs in the warm Caribbean, treading the clearest water over rippled white sand until they find themselves refreshed farther out in cooler water, in the deep *blue reef-scarred sea.*

They knew me as one who asked another volunteer if she would mind holding Creamsicle, a young vanilla and orange pup, while I cleaned his soiled kennel and made his bed at the end of a night. I knew that Katerina would leave the shelter in minutes for the hospital nearby where her father was about to die. She rocked the sleepy pup in her arms. She said, "You are working too fast." She kissed the pup. She handed him to me. She said to me, "You should take your time." We were both tired, and took turns holding the pup against our hearts. They saw this; they knew this. The ward went quiet. We took our time.

The Doll To

*I*n a room in Greensboro, North Carolina, a tornado of dolls touches down. Dolls form the spout and darken the room with all that has been pulled into the funnel of dolls that has sucked up also a telephone, a xylophone, and the dolls are either whole or missing limbs, missing eyes, or have eyes locked open and hair on end. They are naked and clothed, new and old. The dolls that can talk are not talking; the dolls that can "wet" are dry. The cloud of dolls is somehow suspended from the ancient factory ceiling on the third floor of a building that, if it ever caught fire, would go up like that.

The dolls are no longer dolls; they are weather, storming into a room in the town where, down the street, a famous Woolworth's five-and-ten is a civil rights museum, the lunch counter preserved where four black students waited to be served on the first day of February 1960. You buy a ticket to get in to see it, and you buy a ticket for the Doll Tornado, and it's worth the price of admission, both times, to see what is commonplace now as it thunders back down.

I Stay with Syd

I wasn't the only friend Syd's married man hit on the time he came to see her at the beach. I could see he was going to adhere. So I did not want to talk to him. But then Syd had friends over the night before he was going home, and he invited me out west, said, "Why not this over here"—he meant me—"and that over there"—Syd—"not mingling, not taking anything away from each other?

"An amplitude!" he said.

After I turned down the married man, he brought Syd over, gave her a stagy kiss, then turned to me and said, "You're really something." I thought, What a hedge—why not just say you hate me? The striking part of his communication is what he doesn't say, when saying something would make a difference. A passivity.

I went out onto the dock and examined a collection of shells. I like to say "conch" as much as I can. "Dumb conch." Then home to attend to the business end of a sleeping pill.

Between them it was always almost over, especially at the start. Start to finish, had they done all they might have, might have taken what—a month at most? But for Syd it was a romance like a movie by she couldn't think who. So they drew it out and one week each month I moved into the house at the beach.

I have lived here for so long. Here, and not here.

There's a storm blowing in from the south and I'm worried a tree will fall on the house. But I'm worried about that even when it isn't raining. Syd won't pay what the tree man wants to prune the old oak. "Then at least move your bed," the tree man said.

But it is not my bed to move. It is Syd's bed, Syd out west again to visit the married man who wants her to be faithful to him.

Syd returns from the married man and wakes up in the night in tears and does not know why.

"Because you are lonely and empty inside and nothing helps?" I said, and she said, "Yeah, that too."

I stay with Syd her first night back.

The storm makes landfall the night after she returns, and she says we might ride it out in a movie, so we drive to the old theater in the next town over, down the block from the good pizza place, and we sit too close to the screen. The air-conditioning comes and goes. The lobby had already run out of Coke before Syd could place her order.

The preview was a sci-fi thriller, big on effects. Across the screen: COMING IN SEPTEMBER! Then the lights came up, and a police officer ushered everyone out of the theater, said there was a bomb threat.

We stood with a hundred other people across the street from the theater. We were not offered passes for another night, so we figured we might get back in. Only one police car showed up. Several people left to get beer and pizza. We could smell the ocean, even in the rain. My hair was thickened with salt water. Syd pressed a white spot into my sunburned shoulder and said, "Is there an SPF higher than fifty?"

The scent of fertilizer carried from the nursery down the road where you can spend time deciding among identical flats of annuals.

Thirty minutes, and the head of the unconvincing bomb squad, his bored partner returned to the patrol car, told us we could go inside.

Most of the original audience went in and found seats. We sat farther back this time. No reason.

The projectionist started over from the beginning with the same coming attraction, the sci-fi snooze. "Now we're getting nowhere," Syd said.

She put an arm around my shoulder and we settled down to watch.

COMING IN SEPTEMBER!

Hurry up, summer, and end.

The Chicane

When the film with the French actor opened in the valley, I went to the second showing of the night. It was a hip romantic comedy, but it was not memorable in the way his first film had been, the bawdy picaresque that made his name.

More than thirty years ago, my aunt Lauryn had been hired to accompany him on interviews and serve as interpreter. She was a student at the university in Madrid, taking a junior year abroad from her home in the States, in the American Midwest.

Lauryn was lively and funny, a passionate girl with evenly tanned skin. The actor remained in character, and when she wrote him a month later to say that she was late, she did not hear anything back. On the day she miscarried, her best friend thousands of miles away had "a bad feeling" and called the concierge of Lauryn's building in Madrid, otherwise Lauryn would not have survived the overdose.

She rallied with the help of her mother in Chicago, during lengthy conversations she relied on every night. One year later, she met someone who adored her. She had moved to Lisbon to translate medical documents while she completed her last college courses. Macario was next.

*

Macario was in line at the door when the Banco de Portugal opened at nine o'clock. Inside, he took a seat in the partitioned office of a personal banker while the banker secured the key to the strongbox. The personal banker escorted him to the vault, and the two men stood together as Macario unlocked the strongbox and added to its contents a tape cassette in a navy felt bag. He closed the box, and let the banker accompany him upstairs, and to the door.

The bank was in Lisbon, and the trip in from Estoril had taken half an hour. Another driver would make the trip in an hour, but Macario had raced cars for a living, and though semiretired from the circuit, drove with speed and aggression still. Racing was how he had first met Lauryn, an American girl studying languages abroad, who cut classes to go to the track. She looked Latin, not midwestern, and when he saw her at the finish line, he was pleased to find that she was fluent in Portuguese.

When Lauryn brought him home to meet her mother a couple of months later, Hillis wished her husband were alive to help. She was tired from losing her husband not yet a year before, and she made a decision to wish for her daughter's happiness if she could not count on Lauryn's judgment. The wedding was held in Lisbon, with a brief honeymoon at the Ritz. Hillis did not make the trip, but sent a surpassingly generous gift.

The house Macario rented for them in Estoril faced the sea. Chalet Esperanza had been built in the sixteenth century; its terraces poured bougainvillea to the ground. The newlyweds drank coffee in the morning on the bedroom terrace, close enough to the sea to spot starfish on the beach at low tide. Macario brought his bride a tiny poodle—mostly poodle—that had hung around the track for several days. The pit crews had fed it, but no one had showed up to look for it. Lauryn named the little dog Espe; she bathed her and bought the dog a wardrobe of collars. Macario took that summer to get to know his bride.

Lauryn wrote to Hillis about the blissful days they woke to. She told her mother that she walked to the market earlier than the tourists, said she was not herself a tourist since her wedding to Macario. She said she rid herself of the flat Chicago "a"—she noticed this the few times she spoke her native language. She was where she was meant to be, she said, living a life that made sense.

She was learning the history of the coastal towns, visiting the landmark churches, thriving in Estoril's moderate summer instead of the humid heat of Illinois. She said she liked to linger in Parede, a small beach where the high iodine content in the water was said to be good for the bones; there were two orthopedic hospitals in the town. Lauryn told her mother she thought she might visit one and read to the patients in the children's ward.

Some days she went to Tamariz, the beach beside the Estoril Casino and Gardens, or to Praia dos Pescadores for the fish market, or to the baroque Church of the Navigators to pray that Macario would always return to her but not to the track.

Amy Hempel

The Circuito Estoril at the Autódromo was a tricky course on the Formula 1 circuit with its bumpy straights, constant-radius corners, heavy braking zones, and a tricky chicane. The month they had the chalet, July, was a month when only motorbikes raced. Unless Macario and Lauryn extended their stay, his racing pals would not be around to tempt him back onto the course.

Each felt the other was a prize, so where was the need to continue to compete?

Such was Lauryn's thinking, as reported to her mother, and passed along to me. Macario, she pointed out, had filled a trophy case already; did he need to risk his life now that he had a wife and, soon, a child?

Though Lauryn was twenty-one years old, and I was seventeen, she treated me not like her older sister's child, but as someone who could profit from all that she had learned. Though I could not pick up languages the way that she could, I took in other lessons.

That summer, Lauryn started to wear loose shifts. She no longer tucked in her shirts. She took naps, and was alternately sick and ravenous. She instilled in Macario a sense of dynasty, a word she used ironically, but which he did not.

Then she made the classic mistake of taking the exotic out of its element. She took her husband home and turned him into what she could easily have found without leaving Illinois. Macario did not hold it against her, but Lauryn came to blame him for the same things that drew her to him first.

38

After the month in Estoril, Lauryn brought Macario home again. She wanted an American doctor, she wanted her mother's help with the baby, she wanted Macario to take a job with the company her father used to run. She wanted an American husband, after all. When their son, James, was born, Macario pronounced it "Zhime." Portuguese was the language they fought in.

The first two years of motherhood were a balm for Lauryn. During the pregnancy she had stopped taking medication to lift her spirits, and she did not take it up again after the baby was born. She attributed her changes in mood to the new responsibilities, to the vigilance required to protect her child and make sure he would thrive. She talked to her mother on the phone or saw her every day. I saw her every few months when I flew in from California to get away from the life that had not yet started for me. I preferred her life, the one she talked about from before the baby was born.

Macario helped with childcare when he came home from the office in the evening. Still, Lauryn said she needed a break from them all, from it all, and booked a flight to Lisbon on her twenty-third birthday.

*

Macario would not have known there *was* a tape if the chief of police had not been an old friend who told him. It was not generally known that the police taped international calls placed within the capital. So when Lauryn placed the call to her mother in Chicago from a room in the Lisbon Ritz on the last night of her life, the conversation was recorded by police. The chief of police not only told Macario this, he gave him a copy of the tape.

Macario listened to it once, and then put it in his strongbox at the bank. He did not tell Hillis there was a tape of the last conversation she had had with her daughter, or that he had listened to Lauryn as she made less and less sense after taking the pills. But he did tell me.

*

Hillis and I drank coffee on her terrace on the eighteenth floor of her apartment building, close enough to Lake Michigan to smell diesel fuel. She had mostly quit caffeine when Lauryn died; it fought the medication she had taken since then to calm her. But you could not lose everything at once, she maintained, and continued to drink coffee in the morning, as before. In the years since Lauryn died, she had lost her view from the terrace. It had been largely blocked by the John Hancock Building, which she had watched go up from her living room across from the office and residential tower.

Hillis did not want to talk about Lauryn, but she seemed to enjoy my visits when I came back to Chicago from the coast. Though there was not any glamour to the work that I did, my grandmother asked for particulars. In an uneasy near coincidence, I edited articles for medical publications. It was a job I knew I would leave as soon as something better appeared.

I am sure that if Lauryn had wanted a doctor to come and pump her stomach she would have phoned the front desk of the Ritz Hotel and told them to send one up to her room. She wanted to talk to her mother, and hear her mother tell her from thousands of miles away that James was sleeping in the guest room in his crib, and that it was hard to make out what she was saying—could she speak up?—and that she would feel better when she woke up in the morning, and then ask her mother to stay on the line while she sang herself to sleep.

Macario did not let me listen to the tape; I had to take his word for what was on it when he took me aside at James's tenth birthday party and gave me this ugly gift. Why tell me then? He had no answer when I asked him.

This morning I thought to make a tape recording of my own. I wanted to tell my aunt about the party I went to in Malibu last night. The fellow who answered the door was not the host but the French actor, the rake who played a rake in his film debut, who seduced my aunt in Madrid so many years before. He had aged pretty well; he still had it, I thought.

I had wanted to play something out, so I trailed him through the house, then asked if he would step outside and show me the night sky. I introduced myself as Lauryn, and spelled out where the "y" replaced the "e." Did I expect him to flinch? With his arm around my shoulders, he narrated what we looked up and saw. I would not have known if he was right about the constellations. His accent almost worked on me. But when he stopped talking, and leaned in for the kiss, I ducked and said, "You can remember me as the girl you showed the new moon to."

41

"But, darling," he said, "there's a new moon every month."
Still, I wanted to tell my aunt. The days of tape cassettes were
over, but the equipment must be somewhere to be found, and
when I was the one who found it, wouldn't I record a tape on
which I told her the story? Wouldn't I mail it off to Macario
in a suitable felt bag so he could take it to the bank in Lisbon
and unlock the strongbox and place it beside the tape of his
wife chattering away in the vault?

Greed

Mrs. Greed had been married for forty years, her husband the cuckold of all time. A homely man with a notable fortune, he escorted her on errands in the neighborhood. It was a point of honor with Mrs. Greed to say she would never leave him. No matter if her affection for him was exceeded by her devotion to others. Including, for example, my husband. If she was home at night in her husband's bed, did he care what she did with her days?

I was the one who cared.

Protected by men, money, and a lack of shame, Mrs. Greed had long been able to avoid what she had coming. She had the kind of glee that meant men did not think she slept around, they thought she had joie de vivre; they thought her a libertine, not a whore.

She had the means to indulge impetuous behavior and sleep through the mornings after nights she kept secret from her friends. She traveled the world, and turned into the person she could be in other places with people she would never see again.

She was many years older than my husband, running on the fumes of her beauty. Hers had been a conventional beauty, and I was embarrassed by my husband's homage to it. Running through their rendezvous: a stream of regret that they had not met sooner.

He asked if she had maternal feelings for him. She said she was not sure what he wanted to hear. She told him she felt an erotic mix of passion and tenderness. If he wanted to think the tenderness maternal, let him.

When they met, he said, he had not hidden the fact that she looked like his mother, a glamorous woman who had been cruel to him and died when he was a boy. He had not said this to underscore her age, nor did she think it a fixation. She would have heard it as she felt it was intended: as a compliment, an added opportunity to bind them together. She would have been happy to be the good mother, as well as the ultimate sensate. And see how her pleasure seeking brought pleasure to those around her!

A thing between them: green apples. Never red, always green. I knew when my husband had entertained Mrs. Greed because a trio of baskets in the kitchen would be filled with polished green apples. My husband claimed to like the look of them; I never saw him eat one. As soon as they started to soften and turn brown, I would throw them out. And there would be the baskets filled so soon again.

He told me he got them from the Italian market in town. But I checked, and the Italian market does not carry green apples. What the green apples mean to them, I don't know, don't want to know. But she brought them each time she entered our house, and I felt that if I had not thrown the rotting ones out, he would have held on to every one of them. The way he fetishized these apples—it made him less attractive to me.

Mrs. Greed convinced her young lover, my husband, that she was "not the type" to have "work" done, but she had had work done. She must have had a high threshold for pain. She could stay out of sight for the month or more of healing after each procedure. She had less success hiding the results of other surgeries. She claimed her athleticism had made it necessary, claimed a "sports injury" to lessen the horror of simple aging. But she could not hide the stiffness that followed, a lack of elasticity that marked her an old woman who crossed the street slowly in low-heeled shoes. I watched her cross the street like this, supported by my husband.

Maybe that was why she liked to hear complaints about his other women, that they were spoiled and petty, gossips who resented his involvement with her. Because he would not keep quiet about such a thing. At first, she felt the others had "won" because they could see him at any time. Then she saw that their availability guaranteed he would tire of them. They were impermanent, and she knew it before they did. So however much he pleaded with her to leave her husband, or at least see *him* more often, Mrs. Greed refused. It galled me that he wanted her more than she wanted him.

I listened to them often. I hooked up the camera to the computer when I was at home alone. For two hundred dollars I'd bought a hidden surveillance camera that was fitted into a book. I did not expect it to work. I left it next to the clock on the nightstand. I did not pay the additional seventy-five dollars that would have showed them to me in color. But the ninety-degree field of view was adequate for our bedroom, and sound came in from up to seven hundred feet. Had this not worked so well, I would have stood in line for the camera that came hidden in a ceiling-mounted smoke detector.

Usually the things they said were exchanges of unforeseen delight, and riffs of gratitude. But the last time I listened to them, my husband said something clever. Mrs. Greed sounded oddly winsome, said she sometimes wished the two of them had "waited." My husband told her they could *still* wait—they could wait a day, a week, a month—"It just won't be the *first* time," he said.

How she laughed.

I said to myself, "I am a better person!" I am a speech therapist who works with children. Parents say I change their lives. But men don't care about a better person. You can't photograph virtue.

I found the collection of photographs he had tried to hide. I liked that the photos of herself she brought to him were photos from so long ago. Decades ago. She wears old-fashioned bathing suits aboard sailboats with islands in the faded background. Let her note that the photographs of me that my husband took himself were taken in this bed.

Together, they lacked fear, I thought, to the extent that she told him to bring me to dinner at her house. With her husband. Really, this was the most startling thing I had heard on playback. Just before the invitation, she told him she would not go to bed with the two of us. My husband was the one to suggest it. As though the two of us had talked it over, as if this were something I wanted. I heard her say, "I have to be the queen bee." Saw her say it.

She would not go to bed with us, but she would play hostess at dinner in her home.

I looked inside my closet, as though I might actually go. What does one wear for such an occasion? The corset dress? Something off the shoulder? Something to make me look older? But no dress existed for me to wear to this dinner. The dress had to do too much. It had to say: I am the sexy wife, and I will outlast you. It had to say: You are no threat to my happiness, and I will outlive you.

*

Down the street from our house, a car waited for Mrs. Greed. I knew, because I had taken note before, that a driver brought her to see my husband when I visited clients out of town. Was there a bar in the back of this car? I couldn't tell—the windows had a tint. Maybe she would not normally drink, but because there was a decanter of Scotch and she was being driven some distance at dusk, maybe she poured herself a glass and toasted her good luck?

This last thought reassured me. How was it this felt normal to me, to think of her being driven home after a tumble with my husband? I guess it depends on what you are used to. I knew a man who found Army boot camp "touching," the attention he received from the drill sergeant, the way the Army fed him daily. It was a comfort to him to know what each day would bring.

I felt there could be no compensation for being apart from my husband. Not for me, and not for her.

I knew I was supposed to be angry with *him*, not with her. She was not the first. She was the first he would not give up. But I could not summon the feelings pointed in the right direction. I even thought that killing her might be the form my *self*-destruction took. Had to take that chance. I tried to go cold for a time—when I thought of him, when I thought of her. But there was a heat and richness to what I conceived that made me think of times I was late to visit a place that my friends had already seen. When you discover something long after others have known it, there is a heady contentment that comes.

What I heard on the tapes after that: their contentment, their conversation one that we had not been having. Watching them on camera I thought: What if I'm doing just what I'm supposed to be doing? And then I thought: I am.

*

The boys said they would give me a sign.

It was money well spent. With what I saved not needing to film in color, and knowing I would not need the standard two-year warranty, I had enough to pay the thuggish teens a client's son hung out with. The kid with the stutter had hinted he needed m-m-money. I will even give them a bonus—I will let them keep the surveillance camera hidden in the book after they send me the final tape.

Mrs. Greed does not live so far away that I will miss the ambulance siren.

And what to make of this? The apples my husband "bought," the green ones from the Italian market that does not carry green apples—I ate one on the front steps of our house and threw the core into pachysandra. The next morning the core I had thrown was on the top step where I had been sitting when I ate it. I threw it again, this time farther out, so it lodged in pine needles alongside the road in front of our house. The morning after that, today, the core was back in place on the top step.

Boys.

I thought: Let's see what happens next.

We have so many apples left.

Fort Bedd

The second "d" is silent.

We agreed on that, if not on much else.

In a darkened apartment on the west side of the park, when things went wrong, I thought about trees. I wanted lilacs and chestnuts, an Onward pear. Dogwood and silver maple. A copper beech so old that the bench built around it is splintered and gray. Trees take root, and I thought I could too—if I had enough trees to learn from.

"You'll tell me," he said, "if I start to talk crazy.

"If I do something crazy, you'll tell me," he said.

He was incurable; old age can't be cured. We clung to each other for safety in the only safe place we knew. In the dark back bedroom, Fort Bedd the temperature of skin and air, we propped ourselves up on feather-filled pillows, and the wagons circled, but the wagons were pillows too, so Fort Bedd changed its borders with every move we made.

The dark apartment rustled in the dark, and it was dark in the day as well.

There would have been light if the curtains were opened. But they were his curtains to open, and he chose to keep them closed. Sometimes when we had kicked off the pillows and he was asleep, I would walk to the window and yank back the

search2Please

drapes the way an amateur diver might surface too quickly: bubbles in the blood, pain in the joints, then the hyperbaric chamber of Fort Bedd.

If we were going to get through this, I would need trees. The next day, or any day, I could slip away and drive to a nursery, pick out a tree—balled and burlapped—and put it in my car and take it to the edge of a field where no one would see me dig with the shovel I brought along. I could visit the tree I planted, bring water if it needed water. If there was dogwood blight that season, I could plant Pendulum spruce instead.

Plant windbreak, woods, a forest, a glen.

Four Calls in the
Last Half Hour

The relaxed relentlessness, the air of impersonal intimacy, that sense they create of having just been with you despite not having been with you for quite a while; of resuming a rolling conversation that you have not, in fact, been having, that was broken off rather dramatically, actually, by definitive pledges by both parties. They know this, surely, but maybe they're so lonely they don't care—and so grandiose that they think if they don't, you won't. Either that or they're living in another dimension, a dimension you thought that you could live in too, once. Just take me there. Just teach me the rules. You adore them for having a hundred percent of something that you have only sixty-five of, but see that most people have even less of, which is why most people don't interest you much. If the one hundred percent you're transfixed by will sacrifice a fraction of his endowment and you can add a little bit to yours, you'll both be at a formidable ninety percent—approximately equally exalted, since you'll be further than average folks can ever dream of being. You'll be set then. The reigning couple in a private cosmos that's the best little private cosmos out there, because it's yours, all yours, and the humor there is all yours, as well as the sex, the talk, the everything. But the one with

59

one hundred percent won't compromise and soon the eager apprentice just gives up, haunted by images of what could have been if the other had just been flexible. Which he can't be, because he's inflexible and doesn't have to be, because he feels he has it all already and doesn't get lonely the way we do, so why trade self-sufficiency for company. But he does get a little bored sometimes, especially on chilly weekend nights. So he picks up the phone to call one he denied. He picks up the phone again.

The Correct Grip

A few days after the attack, the wife of the stranger who attacked me called me on the phone. She wanted to know if I was serious about her husband. She said he told her he was having an affair with me. She said she got my number from Student Services.

"Your husband broke into my apartment," I said, in the uninflected voice that had taken me this far. "He threatened me with a knife."

"Did he use it?" his wife asked.

"He used it to threaten me," I said.

"Because he used it on me once," she said conversationally. "I have a scar on my forehead like a quarter moon.

"What do you look like?" she asked.

I told her! I played down my looks, but not so far that she would think that was what I was doing.

"You could be describing me," she said, sounding pleased.

She said, "I guess why I'm calling you is to see if I should stay and try to make it work."

I told her I could not possibly advise her, and gave her instead the number of a women's shelter in case he gave her more trouble. I reminded her what her husband had done to me.

She said, "Would you like to have lunch sometime anyway? My treat."

I told her I was moving out the next week. Saying so, I meant it.

I hung up and looked for my dog's new leash.

The phone call I got before the attacker's wife was from a friend who had stumbled on an exposed tree root the day before, had fallen and broken her ankle.

This was in the woods near her house, she said. She told me she had unleashed her retriever and sent him to get help. The dog had returned with a neighbor who called for an ambulance on his cell phone.

I told her that my dog would have done the same thing for me, only stopping first to knock over trash cans and try to get laid.

I was dismayed by my impulse to make fun of rescue. But there is something so convenient about rescue. Yet would I not have been spared if the man who attacked me had been made to drop the knife because my dog had been with me and had pinned him to the ground?

I found the new leash, and set out to walk my dog. In the correct grip, the right thumb goes through the loop in the leather before the right hand doubles over to clutch the extra length. This ensures maximum control and should obviate the need to use the left hand. The correct grip causes the dye in the leather to rub off in the creases of the hand. It strengthens the hand when you form a fist for when the proverbial pendulum swings the hell back.

The Second Seating

The three of us were taken with the vodka fizz made with elderflower and basil so we stayed on and had the raw kale salad and heirloom tomatoes with medallions of halloumi. These were such that we ordered the scallops, and then the frozen chocolate crème brûlée. We had had to arrive early and flag a table outside to get to order anything at all, so by the time we had finished dinner, the sun was still showing through trees near the bay. The day before had been rain all day, so we were satisfied to stay in our seats and take in the scents from the well-tended garden surrounding the lodge.

Bob, dying, had made us promise we would have dinner there without him in the same way he'd told his wife to go ahead with plans to add a screened porch to their house—so there would be one room not filled with memories of him.

We had already missed the last ferry to the mainland. We had nowhere else to be. A couple approached our waitress for a table. She told them the second seating had already filled. We could have given up our seats and paid our bill. But we said to the waitress that we wanted to start over. Then we ordered more drinks, and later the cod.

Moonbow

People are getting away with murder, but I can't get away with having a glass of water in bed. I trade sides with my dog, who won't feel what I spilled anyway.

From this side of the bed, I see the moon through the window. It's a full moon with . . . something extra. I've heard about this, but not in upstate New York—in Africa, where the mist from Victoria Falls on the night of a full moon can cause a rainbow to form, a white one—a moonbow. People book vacations to see it.

I head downstairs, and out to the small backyard. Who else is seeing this? And then I see who else: a small brown bear, or maybe it's black. I freeze, trying not to look scared because that's when they attack, I'm told. A bear is moving calmly from the neighbor's yard into mine. He looks up at the moon; we look at it together. The bear drops to the ground and then stands up pawing a ball. It belonged to my dog, the other one, who died the month before. The bear sees the dog's water bowl I've kept filled from habit or hope, and helps himself to a drink. He wraps himself in the rope from the old tie-out. He swipes at the gone dog's favorite plush toy, a damp, matted lamb with the squeaker torn out.

The bear rolls on his back under the freakish white rainbow, his feet like those of one other creature I knew. "Logan?" I ask, moving a step closer. "It's all right."

I tell him what has happened since I lost him, and assure him that I approved of his valedictory bite, that awful deliveryman who had it coming. I tell him that the deli has gone up for sale, that another antiques store has opened, that I hate my haircut, that I have not thrown anything away, that the water in the kitchen has developed a metallic aftertaste.

And then the bear is leaving. On his feet, and moving to the back of the yard, he stops by the old rope swing. I think he's going to put his legs through the tire and push off toward the moon, but then I see he's got the rope between his teeth. He chews and shakes his head until he has chewed through the rope and the tire falls to the ground, where the bear kicks it out of his way as he tears off through the woods.

Equivalent

*T*he former owner was supposed to fix the door. Instead, he left behind a pool-cleaning robot. He said it was equivalent to fixing the front door, though the house had no pool. It had once had a pool, but the seller's wife had been the swimmer, and when she died four years earlier, he filled in the pool.

At the closing, the buyer's attorney pointed out that the repair of the door was contractually bound. She brought out the contract and showed him. He said you just had to put some shoulder to it. The buyer wanted the house, so she was the one both sides knew would give in.

Every couple of months, the seller arrived unannounced to pick up something he had left behind: a wall phone in the den, canoe mounts in the shed. The buyer allowed him to take what he wanted, then asked for help with a difficult chore. She asked him to turn the mower on its side to drain the oil. And double-check the basement's radon remediator. Each favor she asked extended the time until the seller's next visit. The weeds in the garden—the buyer bets that this will be enough to keep the seller from coming back to get the child's blackboard in an upstairs bedroom, the child's name formed by animals carved in the wooden frame.

The Quiet Car

*T*hat reminds me of when I knew a romance was over. I had not seen this fellow in a while, but he suggested we meet up at the train station and take the Acela somewhere, so I thought we'd have several hours to catch up. And then at the station, we boarded and he led me to our seats in the Quiet Car.

I was glad to have the rented falling-down house through the summer. It was a bicycle ride from the beach, and the owner had let me paint the bedroom a grayish green from the Benjamin Moore Serenity Collection. The floors were sandy even before I went to the beach. There was no pool, but I still might buy the raft that is a giant vinyl slice of watermelon.

The snowbirds are back as of this holiday weekend, not that they are the ones hurling M-80s. The president would have us believe the hurlers of M-80s are members of MS-13; supposedly this little hamlet is their base. But I have been here nearly a year, and have seen no one threatening. I'm the almost retiree who does not go south for the winter. On the mantel, though the fireplace doesn't work, I've propped the housewarming present from a friend: a small painting of a house that is on fire. It's a good painting.

It's fancy camping here, with a refrigerator that freezes food as quickly as the freezer compartment. It can't be fixed, said the repairman who tried on four occasions and then refused to let me pay him. My brother, who owns a bakery in the city, is going to visit next week during a convention. I found that the vegetable drawer is the one part of the refrigerator that will chill instead of freeze, so I will instruct him to keep his butter and cream there. He will examine the failed appliance and ask me if I'd thought to "run the adapter for the RL247 through the Omega conductor or the AcuRite barometer." It's a running gag, that he understands the work of an electrician. I'll say, "Yeah, the first one."

On this holiday weekend, there is a sale on large appliances at Home Depot. I cut the ad out of a circular and sent it to the owner of the house. I bought packets of wildflower and zinnia seeds, and sprinkled them around the falling-down house. Maybe the rain we can expect tonight will do something about it.

Yesterday, where someone had dumped a cat-scratched leather recliner in the weedy empty lot around the corner, an elderly man was found sitting in the chair, quietly disoriented. The recliner looked like a seat on an Amtrak train, in Coach. The man did not seem to know where he was, or how he got there, but he was not fearful, just quiet. He was able to recite his son's email address and list the son's many accomplishments to the police whom someone called to help. They were kind when they contacted the man's son in another state. But this won't go well, I thought, and chose not to follow the story.

Cloudland

And the children in the apple-tree
Not known, because not looked for . . .

—T. S. Eliot, *Four Quartets*

/ remember thinking: There will never come a time when
I will not be thinking of this. And I was right. And I
was wrong.

*

The locals say that in Florida, you have to go north to be in the
South. It is January and seventy-five degrees, and there are
citrus trees in the yard. Tomorrow I am going to pick pounds
of kumquats from one of those trees, and make marmalade
from a recipe that requires me to procure a twenty-quart pot
and a set of tongs to lift boiled-sterile jars from the boiling
water, and another tool to secure the lids to the jars. This if
the pectin does its job and the shredded kumquats cohere
without forming clumps. I already know that something
as simple as a longish wait at a stoplight on the way to the
"culinary arts" store for the above will be enough to send me

back home to admire the kumquats dotting the lush tree, and never take a step closer to pick them.

No one expects me to make such a thing. Aren't there whole stores devoted to the sale of marmalade? Whole malls of marmalade, and not just from this country? I thought it would be fun to surprise a few people. Though there are other ways to surprise them, and probably a better idea not to surprise anyone at all. I know I have had all the surprise I can take.

"Happy New Year," people call out wherever one goes.

Sure, I'll play along: "Happy New Year," I say back.

Had the last year ended?

What if you are someone who does not know when something is over? What if you are the last one standing when others have left the concert, the theater, the crime-addled city, the busted love affair? What if you look for a sign and a sign doesn't come. Or a sign comes but you miss it. What if you have to make a decision on your own and it feels like a body blow, falling back on yourself.

*

I get by working two to three days a week, and not even a whole day at that. There is no state income tax in Florida, housing costs are low, and after a four-week course of study I had a certificate that allowed me to sign with an agency that sends me to private homes and "senior" communities where, as a home health aide without an RN, I can wash people's bodies and help them get dressed; I can take a temperature and wrap a cuff around an arm—sitting, then standing—to get blood pressure readings. I get groceries and do laundry, and heat up soup and make a grilled cheese sandwich. No chance of the sleeve of a patient's robe brushing the flame of a gas burner. I can show a family member, if a patient has one who visits, how to reposition their relative to avoid strain on the back. I keep records of new things I notice about my patients. Not trained or certified to diagnose or prescribe, I can at least render clear descriptions of what I see that was not there before. That is all the responsibility anyone should want me to have. It's no matter; there is dignity in work.

A woman of her word can do what she signed on to do. As I do now with those in my quasi-professional care. I'm a good listener, I'm told, so I get asked back; the agency is glad for the good word-of-mouth. I find the work easy and pleasant, unless someone with a frontal lobe injury acts out. Mr. Davis, that is, an eighty-year-old newly moved into assisted living after he went on a cruise to Alaska with a friend. About to go into bankruptcy, he opened a line of credit aboard the ship to buy a diamond ring with which he proposed to the captain's wife. He still feels misunderstood: "Everyone likes to be flirted with," he insists every time I visit.

I could not live on this salary outside of Florida. Which is largely why I moved here from New York. Too young to retire, I left the profession of teaching English in high school—a good, private school for girls in Manhattan—in a denouncement of ambition. That is the way I tell it. All these women

85

breaking glass ceilings, and I found one firmly in place. Not to suggest that helping older people manage is not a valuable use of time. But it was not a calling for me; it was a default position, something I could nominally train for that would barely support me after feeling that I had been ambushed, though what happened was entirely my fault; I had gone off the tracks.

Parents are cautioned against becoming their children's friends. They are meant to be parents, and make unpopular decisions for the well-being of their children. But teachers are not warned against this, and I was a friend to many of my students. So when I invited some of them to my apartment for tea, and one of them produced cocaine, and I had a tiny bit right along with them, I did not blame the girl who reported this to the headmistress. I was allowed to leave without charges being filed, though there would not be a reference should I want to teach elsewhere.

I left quietly, moved out of state. I still wanted to be of use, hence the four-week preparation to do the job I now do, with no interest in advancement. I drove to Florida in my old Toyota Camry that still had the bumper sticker I had long ago affixed: I BRAKE JUST LIKE A LITTLE GIRL.

The school where I taught exceptionally bright girls had been able to pay serious writers to come in and talk to them, to read to them and take their questions. For the twenty years that I taught there (my first job after grad school), I insinuated myself into the company of creative people; I asked them what to read, and how to construct a bigger picture of what was available to a person with curiosity and a need—at the time—to be more than she was. Many obliged.

*

I have to be available on short notice every other weekend when the aides with seniority can choose a less intensive schedule. That does not present a problem. I have to give the agency thirty hours a week. In exchange for contracting to do this, the four weeks of training were free; some kind of government grant covered the costs.

My off-hours, which are many, are given to home maintenance. If I had known what would be involved, I would not have rented this house—suspiciously cheap, even by north Florida standards. The owners saw me coming. They saw that I had not lived here before, and so would not know what was normal and what was not when it came to keeping up a place. I had been given a further small reduction in rent for agreeing to keep up the pool in place of the pool company the owners hired. I knew nothing. I said sure. I liked Banana Land—the area off the small patio that was planted with sandy bananas, and frequented by black racers, please God, not a coral.

The neighbor across the street enjoyed telling me that a coral snake had turned up in the woodpile between my house and the one next door, and did not offer to tell me that this happened twelve years earlier; I had to pull it out of him. I could tell he was trying to frighten me so that he could offer to help me out. After I mentioned the flooding from the bathtub my first week there, he showed up at my front door with a length of rusty tubing—a *snake*. He wanted to perform a test on the drain, uninvited. I turned him away, saying the plumber had performed this very test, though I didn't know if he had or not. It took some doing, getting the neighbor, eighty-eight by his declaration, to take away his snake.

One is not supposed to fear the snakes, or the gators, though one must stay clear of them. The latter appear to be sunning themselves, indolent, but they can move suddenly and quickly. They are mascot to a team, to a school, and puns abound: the slogan "For the Gator Good."

But I don't mean to make fun. I like it here. A friend said this once about California—the running joke to make fun of Los Angeles—but he loved the place; he had kicked a habit there. I'd say I'm getting better here, but that might be premature. I am not getting worse is what I should probably say. What's the old song—"You may get better but you'll never get well." It's the name of the song or the refrain. I heard a man play it on a piano in a barn, and a number of other people knew the words to it too.

*

"If something is too good to be true, it is." But maybe I had not yet learned this saying as a girl of eighteen. Or maybe I needed something to be that good. Many people must need something to be good enough to get them out of the worst trouble they have gotten themselves into. Especially when that trouble includes another person, one who had no say.

A former colleague at school said he could imagine himself a father only from the moment he claps a young man on the back and says, "This is my son—he's a freshman at Harvard."

But I was humorless at eighteen. I might have ended things as so many others did. I had no sense of the sanctity of life. I judged no one who did not see it through. The baby's father remained with his family. I loved him, and he loved women, told me he would rather look at a woman than look at the Grand Canyon. So I chose not to tell him what had happened. Sometimes I forget why I did not end it. I think that if I could not find a place I felt at home, I was carrying someone who *was* at home, at least for those months.

I had to take the doctor's word for it. The nurses concurred: the child was a girl. She is healthy, they said, and they carried her from the birth room. It was a scene from a hundred years ago—a young woman not prepared to keep the child, bearing the child in a Maternity Home in the shameful shadow of yore. The mother not allowed to hold the swaddled infant, just left alone in a sweat-soaked bed to find her breath and dry her tears and get her strength back and leave the home without the child, leave the other young women about to do the same. And never learn the names of the people who were going to take them in—these children left behind—though we were required to send the home money for a time to ensure the continuation of care in case they were not chosen to join a family right away.

I never thought I was one for fantasy. I never dreamed up scenarios that could not occur in real life. Instead I replayed moments of previous happiness, glad to be reminded of joy or contentment in a lovely place. The lovely place was usually a beach, one with clear, warm water—the Caribbean. Often I picture myself floating facedown in shallow water the temperature of my skin, eyes open to see the rippled white sand and reach for oblong shells the color of clementines. Places were safe to conjure; there was always the chance of returning to a charmed beach. Less safe to call up a person who could not be reached, would not welcome being reached, and thus set in motion the horror of longing. Which word sounds worse—"longing," or "yearning"? I used them interchangeably when they were what I felt, and felt for a long time.

But a fantasy for someone else is different; it's a kind of conceptual gift. I had given myself over: I was all-out, all-in, when I pictured the life of that child. Sometimes a day at a time, each day of her life, and other times I would let my attention leave a lecture or a play, even a good one, and watch a life play out, a life I had had no way to follow once I made the decision that seemed to me to be the one that was better for her. Oh, and better for me too—no pretending it wasn't better for me, as well.

I pictured her with animals—if not growing up on a farm, then living in a place with dogs and cats. Healthy, of course, with friends who were loyal and parents who did no harm. Parents who could not believe their luck at getting *this* girl to raise, who would give her an heirloom ring when she turned sixteen, not a moment of hesitation in giving her that ring.

I would call up the moments that had made me happy, and I put her in those moments, and savored her responses, and in this way she grew up with me. She was with me in the Michigan dunes of the Upper Peninsula in the summer, in a motorboat on a Great Lake, her adoptive father making room for her to stand at the helm and push the lever up to go faster, and down to slow down. Flies and mosquitoes were unseen in these visions. So were sunburn, seasickness, and fear of deep water when the boat was anchored and the ladder let down in the stern for those not afraid of dark water to swim within range of the boat. Swim and then come back aboard for pink lemonade from a thermos filled at home. And though I was a child who had no use for a life jacket, she is wearing one every time she steps off the ladder into the lake.

*

I have heard jokes about impossible things to joke about: the Holocaust, AIDS, the attack on the Twin Towers. Shouldn't I have heard a joke by now about what I did? Not to say it would be the equal of these horrors. Just that the joke, were there a joke to be made, would have been on me. Would have been at my expense. And rightly so.

*

The night before a freeze, I asked a clerk in a nursery what plants she would recommend I wrap. She told me she had grapefruits and kumquats and Meyer lemons, and she did not plan to wrap any of them. "A freeze will make them sweeter," she said, but it sounded as though she did not want to bother. I don't plan to wrap the kumquat tree in my yard so I can test her claim. There are two kinds of people, the clerk said—those who peel the tart rind off, and those who eat the kumquat whole. The rind is the point, is what I think.

I didn't plant this kumquat tree, of course. The owners of the house did. But why did they stop there? They had four young children, I knew, and wouldn't those children have liked to drink orange juice from their own tree?

Dozens of other trees on the property were cut down as I watched. Three men from the utilities company cut bamboo that reached an electrical wire, that according to them caused an outage that interfered with a neighboring church's mass. Service, I think they meant; it's an Episcopal church. The utilities workers knew nothing about cutting back trees. They butchered them gratuitously, leaving jagged branches and broken limbs for me to clean up. Left broad openings in the protective hedge.

I heard of a man near here who bought ten acres of forest, and one morning discovered that the utilities company had cut a swath across his land, had cleared a huge path in the trees, for no reason he could see. He threatened to sue, and the utilities company said to go ahead and sue. At a certain point, it would seem, you have to stop caring, and stop trying to protect what someone else is set to destroy.

*

It's exhausting to see things grow so fast. That is, if you are trying to maintain separation between nature and a house, are trying to keep what belongs outside, outside. There is no dormant season here, no downtime in which to rest up for spring and the cleaning and purposeful work it calls for. Up north, one raked leaves onto tarps and, with the help of a neighbor, hauled them off to the woods or filled tall, sturdy brown paper bags and lined them up on your lawn near the street for pickup. "Whew. I'm stuffed!" is what's printed on these bags stocked in home improvement stores.

In some neighborhoods here, people on the block that has an abandoned house on it take turns mowing that house's yard.

The most beautiful yard I ever had was near a beach on the East End of Long Island. I had rented the place with three friends for a summer. We let the backyard go, and by August, the long grass was swirled by winds and deer bedding down into patterns that must have been even better seen from above, by tourists in a glider, or in a hot-air balloon, or a pilot slowing to land a small plane on the next town over's airstrip.

*

I am rested enough to be the conduit for pleasing others—donating clothes to a clothes drive, taking a patient's dog to swim in a dog park pond, sweeping the sand off the walkway to the front door. This last will please the neighbor who bicycles over to sell the Lions Club chicken dinners. I point

out the improvements to the easement in case he has not
noticed, since he sometimes drives by after dark.

It would be something if it turned out the Lions Club gave
money to places like the home. But maybe that is the last
place the Lions would support. And now that I have made the
effort to look them up, sure enough, their good works abound.
They collect used eyeglasses to donate as needed, they are a
secular service organization, they figure in disaster relief
as far away as Japan (earthquake victims), they plant trees,
they repair playgrounds, they conduct health screening and
food drives, they help schoolchildren in Uganda.

*

And now people are overcome as they mourn the death of a
genius performer. The sadness is made larger because the
death of Prince was unexpected, and the grief is mixed with
joy—there are pop-up tributes around the world, and people
find themselves surprised by tears, and good works surface
only now because he did not advertise his philanthropy.
I have often given his CDs to patients; even the ones who
already knew his work were glad to have it in hand. You want
to be choosy about what you let into your soul when you are
likely not long for this world.

*

"The geese in chevron flight"—these are Joni Mitchell's
words, and I hope the girl got to see this. In my mind, she
sees this over and over, every year at the right time of year.

The sound is part of the vision, of course, and part of Mitchell's haunting song "Urge for Going." I played it countless times. Sound calls up yearning more than anything you can see, and is why I no longer listen to the much-loved song.

Music: taken. Perfume: taken. Candles: taken. Velvet shirt: taken. Fireplace too. Used to, used to.

You can shut it all down. Every last thing you defined yourself by—you can give it up, and go without, and put up a front that gets some traction. You must keep your gaze turned outward. Pay attention to others. Don't fall back on what is waiting to take you down. Or *choose* to fall back on it, with arms flung out at your sides.

*

Picture a painting of water on a wall—a painting of a lake is framed on a living room wall, and water from that painted lake is coming in the open door. Water is leaking into a corner of the room; it pools and spreads toward the center of the room. The painting is titled *Water Damage*, and the artist got it right. I would be happy to look at this painting every day, and I can; it has been reproduced in a book. I would be the better for it, sharing the artist's vision.

A song with geese in it, a painting with water in it, a person finding treasures that she hopes the child found. Not this particular song, and not this particular painting not yet painted back then, but a song that took the child to the heart of the world, and a sight that summed up much of what she loved.

*

I said I might have ended things as so many others did. Yet I found my way to a kind of haunted house, an old-fashioned mansion in a corner of rural Maine that could have scared people in a movie about a haunted house, and that did, in fact, haunt the women who for a short time lived there, as I did at eighteen. I had gone to Maine to visit a cousin in August. On a sightseeing trip one day, I drove past the farm that sold organic produce, and then past the truck that sold lobsters out of the back on Main Street, and kept going for hours until I entered a small town that felt familiar, though I couldn't think why, something generic about it. Something not welcoming, though that was a lot of places I had been. I parked my car on that drowsy summer day, and set out to see as many houses as I could, to see how people lived there. I walked in the direction that the houses became more grand, older, well preserved, forbidding, until I came to the home. It was dark even in daylight, built not to bring in light but to withstand the storms of winter. The yard—one might say grounds—was neatly kept and simply planted. I didn't know what I was seeing the first time I saw it. Like an exclusive club in the city, there was an address but no name. I felt transfixed by the place, as I had once felt in England seeing a house comparable to this one, but that was on a tour of national historic houses. This one was not a national treasure, nor was it a home. It was a Maternity Home. I did not yet know that I would need the home's services a few months later.

Cloudland

*

The license plate for Maine, since 1936, says VACATION-
LAND. But I never coaxed a kayak down a duck-visited river,
or boiled a lobster, never picked blueberries growing wild
at the side of a road, or wrote my name on a piece of curled
bark. I did collect birch bark when I found it in the orchard
behind the home. The orchard was bounded by birch trees
and a small pond just beyond. Wind would blow loose bark
into the orchard, and if I had been sentimental back then,
maybe I would have chosen a name for the girl and written it
on a piece of bark, and carried it with me ever after. None of
us who gave birth in the home were expected to return, not
to check in about a child or to visit for what some people call
closure. The closure I could expect involves a sign ahead of
a closed lane or exit ramp that says ROAD CLOSURE AHEAD.
I'm always glad those roads have closure.

Not expected to return, not encouraged to stay in touch,
we launched ourselves from the slate front steps of the home
and it was good-bye and not even good luck. Just keep going.

Years later, I became acquainted with the parents of some
of the girls where I taught. One couple, a painter and his
beautiful wife, had bought an old fishing camp on a lake
in the same small inland town where the home had been
located. It had since burned down, for which I was grateful.
The couple had turned the fishing camp into an endless
astonishment of studios and galleries and playrooms, a place
no one wanted to leave. Another parent from the school

invited me to her grand refuge of a house nearby that was built upon rock ledges that hung above a lake. A deck ran the length of the side facing the lake—you would look down and find yourself hanging above dark water.

The painter's wife knew how to cut hair, and said she wanted to volunteer to cut homeless people's hair. She said she thought it would make them feel better. I thought it was a good idea, generous. But the painter cautioned against it, said he didn't think it was a good idea to use scissors and a razor on the heads of people who were, some of them, mentally ill, and distraught. But maybe you could pick and choose, in the interest of safety and good works. Though I guess many of us have been fooled. I have certainly fooled myself, from time to time to time.

The last time I was in Maine, before I left New York for Florida, I saw tourists taking pictures of mallards along a river. One young girl, maybe twelve years old, took pictures of scat, and giggled when she advanced her camera. I liked her right away, a girl I would not see again.

I met a woman who said she conceived *of* her daughter before she conceived her. I was one of the ones for whom it went the other way. I could not conceive of that creature, though she was making her way inside me, not even when the doctor handed her off to a nurse and she was carried out of the room. I was weak from labor, and I was weak with relief. The transaction was not free, but I was free to go.

*

Sometimes I can't bear the responsibility of carrying a purse. I will put a few dollars and a ChapStick in a pocket of my jeans or a pocket of a light canvas jacket, and head out for a walk in the botanical gardens. For an entry fee higher than you might expect, you can walk the paths through native flora, all of it identified by tiny signs. The best thing there is the bamboo garden, the familiar green to ebony and even blue bamboo. There is one kind of plant along the paths that is known as purple heart—it's in the yard of the rented house, and I think more of it now that I know its name. There are signs that designate sinkholes. No cars or pancaked apartment buildings at the bottom—these sinkholes occurred in an open field where visitors can stand behind a low wooden enclosure and look down to where snakes and skinks have staked a claim.

*

I have not told anyone about the girl, so no one knows what I did when she was born. I almost said "taken," but she was not taken, she was given. I gave her for adoption. For safekeeping, for peace of mind.

The staff at the home seemed nice enough, by which I mean that one could meet a nurse's eyes and not feel judged. Those of us who made an arrangement to do so could check in, as to an inn, and stay for as long as we needed before giving birth. We were not pampered, but neither were we deprived of small niceties: lavender-scented soap, fresh—if not ironed—linens, and bedside radios as long as we kept the volume down. There were no locks on the doors of our rooms, but no one seemed bothered by that, at least not when I was there. Unlike some of the others, I did not stay for very long. There was shame attached to being there, coming naturally to some, stirred up in others.

There were no group activities foisted upon us, for which I think all of us were grateful. No mandatory chapel attendance, though there was a small chapel attached to the home (it might have once been an extra bedroom, long since fitted out with pews and stained glass). We were not allowed to eat in our rooms, so breakfast, lunch, and dinner were where we got to know who else was there.

I had spent a few years at boarding school, so I took to the dormitory feel of the place. Others did not like sharing a room, and wore a towel into the shower stall, and slept facing the wall. But for me it was nostalgic to be in a large Victorian house with other young women.

Just a week after I had settled into the home, the morning sickness passed. I thought it was a sign that I had done the right thing. But I had not done the right thing. But I didn't know it yet.

There were times the home seemed empty of people in charge. Where did the nurses go for whole afternoons, and where was the housekeeper who sometimes swept the floors in our rooms? Where was the handyman when a lightbulb burned out at night and a woman still wanted to read? Where were the matron and her husband? None of us knew what the husband was ever up to other than trying to raise money to keep the place going. The matron—old-fashioned name—was not part of the day-to-day; she delegated jobs to the visible staff, and seemed to rely on regular briefings. They seemed like stock characters to me, these stern, shadowy figures in the haunted-feeling house.

We could go where we wanted, not that the small town had much to offer. A buddy system was encouraged but not enforced, in case one were to feel faint from exertion. An unspoken rule was in effect, one that discouraged eliciting personal information. My only complaint was the setting of the thermostat; it was kept to a temperature lower than allowed for coziness at night, or in the day, even given the fact that pregnant women often run hot. One had to rely on old crocheted afghans pulled around hunched shoulders. Some were made from continuous stitches, and some assembled from dozens of pot-holder-like squares. The squares didn't match, and the sight of a pile of these homemade throws could be dizzying.

So little was asked of us. Oh, we were asked for money, but this was not a charity we had come to.

When I said "nurses" before, I didn't mean that we were treated like patients. Our vital signs were not checked, nor prenatal vitamins offered. Unless delivery was imminent they were more like hall monitors or housemothers. We supposed that they kept the matron informed of the smooth, or less than smooth, running of the operation. And on days when the doctor was called in, they proved themselves indispensable. Housemothers became medical professionals, and we guests became mothers.

*

On Thursday afternoons, I check in on the man in his nineties who always has his TV on. This is not uncommon among the people I look after. This fellow likes the show where Realtors show people three houses for sale and the people choose one of them to buy. On the day I'm remembering, the show films in the Caribbean. A broker shows a couple a magnificent house with incomparable views and two infinity pools. The wife takes it all in and says to her husband, "I could never be happy here."

This man in his nineties was once CEO of a large northeastern corporation. I think we hit it off because he told me he had often wished, before heading into a board meeting, that he was a desk clerk in a modest chain motel.

*

"I see a child coming forward." That is what the psychic said to me, the one who said she saw me surrounded by moving boxes (I had just moved to Florida). At the time she said it, I was blank, I saw no one—what child? Then I thought maybe she meant a young girl I was fond of, Lois's ten-year-old granddaughter, who could already pull a face like the best stand-up comic. She had enviable timing, and didn't know she had this power. Though I didn't get to see the girl often, I was moved to want to care for her. The family had its struggles.

It was not until I was driving home that I knew who the psychic saw coming forward. And I had to pull the car over.

Well, I almost pulled the car over. It was that kind of realization. And a measure of the distance I had come from the way I had once felt; there was a gap, and it was only a few minutes, but it hadn't used to be there, not any gap at all.

There was a girl I saw eating a sandwich sitting on the lawn of her house the other day. She wore a turtleneck shirt, and I noticed her because she had put both of her arms through one sleeve of the long-sleeved shirt. She held the sandwich off to the side with both hands while one sleeve flapped in the breeze. I was in a car stopped at a light when I saw her, but even if I had been walking past, I would not have wanted to know why she put both of her arms in one sleeve. She made me smile, a contrast to the boy in a stroller in a crowded market who shoved a handful of fruit into his mouth and then spit out the words "I just can't wait to eat these delicious berries," repeating the act until the box of raspberries was gone. His lack of control or the use of the word "delicious"—it was hard to say which was worse. Three guesses as to whether the mother paid for the empty box.

*

I am never glad to hear from a person I knew a long time ago. What do you want from me—that is the dreaded question—and why now. Though when I heard from one of the women who had been at the home when I was, the usual queasy feeling made room for curiosity. The call came just after I arrived in Florida.

The person who tracked me down was possibly the meekest of the residents at that time. She had suffered from hyperemesis gravidarum, which did not taper off the further along she got; it kept her vomiting for the duration. There was nothing she could keep down beyond the occasional saltine and a few sips of ginger ale, so it was a surprise to us all when her baby was born undamaged. Not that the baby remained *her* baby. This was a boy, we were told. And true to the old saying, this boy had not robbed her of her looks. Sick as she had been, she displayed an odd radiance from the time she arrived to the day she left.

She told me that her brother—conveniently a private investigator—had helped her locate me. She said she wanted to know if I had seen the book. What book? The book about the home, she said.

She said she figured I had not heard about it, that it was published by a small press, and might not have been widely reviewed. She did not want to say more. Or she said more, but she was cryptic. Before she hung up, she told me that if I could not secure a copy on my own she would send her copy to me.

She called on a day that reminded me I needed boots—three inches of rain fell in less than half a day. I found a store that was having a sale. The boots did not have to be stylish, just waterproof.

I tried on a left boot from the display and asked the salesgirl if she could find its mate. She came back with another left boot. She said, "I found it," and handed it to me to try on. When I pointed out that she had brought me a second left boot, she said no, it was for the right foot. I showed her that the toes of both boots turned toward the right. She would not be persuaded. I put on the boot, and it was obvious to me and to a second salesperson I hadn't known was there that I was wearing two left boots. "Let me get you the right one," he said. The salesgirl was not affected by this in any way I could see.

*

It was the policy of the home not to let us see them. It was supposed to be easier this way, but whoever it was easier for, it was not easy for us. Some of the women tried to get around this. Others, myself included, were too tired to make a fuss. We were told that the adoptive parents would pick up the babies in the office, which was on a different floor of the home. It was said to happen almost immediately after a birth; it was that well coordinated, we were told.

Waiting for the book to arrive, I went with some friends to a movie about a long-married couple. The friends had been married as long as the couple in the film. The make-believe husband let a secret erupt, and the whole quiet film showed the effects on the wife of this act. The wife was played by an actress you would want to watch do anything on-screen.

At dinner after the movie, we found we had opposite reactions. My friends thought the woman in the film was awful and unfair; they thought her husband was "lost," and rooted for him. But I thought the husband was selfish, and at fault, and behaved gratuitously badly. He had failed his wife in public at their anniversary party. His comments were inadequate, with all of their friends there to hear them. I sided with the wife in the film, whose long marriage was suddenly in question. My friends defended the keeping of secrets, but I think of secrets as lies.

Is it possible to keep a secret from a psychic? The one who told me she saw a child coming forward, she was one of dozens of psychics in a town famous for them. A couple of hours' drive from here is the tiny old town that was once a spiritualist camp and a paranormal vortex. There is a haunted hotel if you want to stay overnight, and first-rate occult bookstores and crystal shops. I bought a pair of earrings made of green aventurine. I'd hoped a "d" had been left out by accident, but no. Though it's "adventurine" when anyone asks me.

The official T-shirt of Cassadaga shows the name of the town, and underneath it the slogan: Where Mayberry Meets the Twilight Zone.

That's where I live!

The bar in the haunted hotel is where one can wait for a session. I plan to go there again and again, trying different psychics until I find one who won't tell me the truth.

*

I had the great luck to be introduced to a woman of immeasurable kindness and talent who had a remarkable ability to create beauty around her. She is herself a world-class beauty. She is a painter and I love her paintings. She is a most generous friend who gave me the two I loved best. In one, there are three little girls in white dresses. There are no features on their faces. They stand on the shore of an island, waving to whoever is on the boat that is either approaching the island where they stand or leaving it behind. I asked her who the little girls in white dresses were. In her ninetieth year, she told me: "Me, myself, and I." And are the people in the boat they wave to—are these people arriving or leaving? I asked. "Leaving," she said. "The girls are waving good-bye."

In another painting she gave me there are four faceless girls in white dresses. There is a sense of urgency as they flee the storm that is gathering above them; they are trying to get to safety, to leave "Cloudland."

*

What if one could find solace in cleaning? What if I could learn to put a bag inside a vacuum and push it about a room and have the dirt transported just like that. Oh, I know how to vacuum—just what if I could find the Zen component, if there is one to be found, in washing dirty dishes, in bleaching the bowl of a toilet, having first procured a plumber to *fix* that toilet. What if I changed the sheets that have gone unchanged, and swept a porch of pine needles and leaves, used a broom to rid the front door of cobwebs and adhesive beetles, and raked up the pinecones blown down by high winds onto the patchy lawn. Anyone else would have done these things by now. What must it be like to live an ordered life?

A friend from the New York days, the stylish Christopher, lived a life of ease and said to me one day, "When life is easy, it's an easy thing to take a life." He was being provocative,

I think that was what he was being. No way to find out now; years ago the ease went out of his life and he died of AIDS. But isn't it also true that when life is hard, it's easy to take a life? Sometimes the answer is yes when a person asks if it would kill you to get the mail.

*

"Estrogenous." Not even a real word, yet any woman can hear the insult in it. Misogynists use this word, and a doctor used it in the home. It is a way to dismiss a woman and what she says, what she thinks, because she is believed to be overrun with hormones. And although the doctor in the home did not use the word to describe me, I thought less of him for using it at all.

We were there to ride out the wait. The place was not clean, but it was far away from anyone any of us knew, and once we came up with the money, the great deal of money required to be there, we would know that we had provided for the future of the children whom we would not see. We would remember this when everything reminded us of what we had done. That was the best we could do; we had done the best that we could.

But after I received the book, and read it the first time, I was made sick. After I learned what was done in the orchard of the home. Before, when I was there and didn't know, the other women and I would pick up fallen apples in the orchard and bring them inside to place in a large wooden bowl on a milk-painted table inside the back door. The gardener took some of them home to his wife if the cook did not need them

all for the pies that she served after chicken and dump-
lings on Sundays. After reading the book, I was made sick
by apples, by the thought of apples, the word itself, even the
letter "a" as it might end up spelling "apple." Keep them away
from me—the red and the green ones, the ones from Asia that
taste like pears, same goes for those that hide under crusts
in pies. Cider in autumn—not a chance anymore.

The author of the book had been born at the home; her
adoptive parents told her. The author was a journalist, and she
looked into the place. There had been rumors, accusations.
The place had been rebuilt after the fire, and resumed its
shady business for some years more. But things did not add
up. There was the caretaker's confession, another from an
attendant who left shortly after she was hired. The author
was not the first to look into the home, but she was the one
who refused to be turned away. Others had been threatened. No one would cooperate. She kept on, and secured a
confession from a handyman who could no longer live with
himself. He told her that in order to save money, the babies
that were not as likely to be adopted were not fed. They were
not given milk, and they were not given medicine, and that
was the standard operating procedure until these babies
died, and were placed in the miniature coffins for which
wooden butter boxes were repurposed. The handyman had
then buried them in the adjacent orchard.

The author reported on local officials concerned with
child welfare and adoption practices, and those who dedi-
cated themselves to enlightened social welfare—the people

who eventually succeeded in shutting the place down. The author advertised, and was able to locate others who had been born there and were then adopted. They were still being counted, she said. They held reunions. And who was held accountable? Those who should have been punished were already gone, the author wrote.

"Walk it off," the nurses told us when we were strong enough to walk, as we prepared to leave the home.

*

There is a wetlands preserve a couple of miles from my house where, for a small donation, you can walk the beautiful acres that are home to many kinds of birds and wildlife. At the trailhead, there is a whiteboard where hikers can write down what they saw each day. You can expect to see gators, ibis, wood storks, and herons, and one day a joker who preceded me wrote "penguin." On my next pass, under "Sightings," I wrote "children." By the time I returned it had been erased; someone had written "lawyer" and drawn a frowny face beside it. The next time I went to the preserve, I wrote on the whiteboard: "steel horse," and went back later in the day to see if anyone got it, and was glad to see that someone had written two words before and two words after mine, completing the line from Bon Jovi: "On a steel horse I ride." The other sightings on the board that day were common king snake, brahminy blind snake, snake, snake, Chihuahua, snake.

*

This part of Florida—not on the ocean, not on the Gulf—is, for now, exempt from the threat of flooding, though a hurricane will take down trees, and the northern part of town is part of Lightning Alley. "Fecund" is a word that comes to mind, as is the phrase "insects on steroids," one hears that all the time. No tourist season, no real tourists, but people who went to the university often come back on Game Days, so you need to plan a different route to get across town.

There is ease, and one can afford it. The land is flat, there is a small downtown of bars and pretty good restaurants and a good coffeehouse the students hang out in. I live out where the neighborhood developments have names on wooden signs. Though mine somehow lost its sign. If you want an international city, Miami is a four-hour drive south.

It is home for now, but where does one ever feel at home? Thousands of refugees, and I have the luxury to consider this question. If a family from Syria needed this house, I would let them have it. Except then they would have the same problems to fix, and where would they get jobs? Would the children be allowed to attend a local school? For a small part of every day, I look online at houses for rent, here and in other cities. Never mind that I don't have a job in these places, I look at houses and wonder if that might be home.

It is Valentine's Day, and we hear that up north it is so cold that flower vendors are losing a fortune, the flowers freezing before they can be delivered. Which probably boosts sales for purveyors of chocolate. This is either cyclic or a new and ominous development for the planet. A real estate broker tried to interest me in a house on the Gulf coast when I was still looking, and when I asked how many years till it would be underwater, the broker said, "Why bring up the controversy?" Climate change is the controversy. The broker said it had not hurt sales at any of the beaches yet, not even Miami or St. Pete, expected to be the first to go under.

I don't need flowers or chocolate today, but because I need a pick-me-up and am not carrying cash, I drive over to the college campus, where, planted throughout, there is a kind of holly called yaupon, the berries of which are poisonous, but if you chew a handful of leaves they work on you like caffeine.

Half an hour's drive from my house is a prison town; the prison is a serious one, at that. Put to death there?—Ted Bundy, for one. It's not a town where you want to stop for gas, and you'll get a ticket for driving two miles over the limit. I've only known one person who was imprisoned, a guy I went out with once. He was smug, I thought, but this was back when I gave people a chance. We met up at a movie theater, and had to wait in line for half an hour.

"Lucky I brought something to read," he said. Ha! What a dick. Not long after, I heard he was doing time for embezzlement. Asked myself: Going to learn this time? Okay, another time. Next time.

*

The climate change nonbeliever across the street stops by on a weekday morning to ask if it is a good time "for a little neighborly chat." I'm late to visit a patient, and tell him I'm getting ready to go to work, but when he turns away with an apology, I make the effort and ask how he's doing. He's going to be ninety in a week, he says, which is impressive since he so recently told me he was eighty-eight. Plus I know what the neighborly chat will be about—he has made other neighbors believe that we are close, so they have deputized him to speak to me about the yard. He would be within his rights to speak to me about the mailbox tumped over on its post. How quickly this place could become the neighborhood eyesore. It's already worse than when I moved in. The house that someone died in at the corner is in better shape than this one, and it is kept up by the grandchildren who live in Colorado.

The day before the neighbor's visit, what a scare! I was dog-sitting Lois's Samoyed, and he jumped the fence and disappeared. A kind woman found him wandering alone and saw the number on his tag. She phoned to tell Lois he was safe nearly a mile away. Lois gave her my number, and she offered to drop him off for me as she would be heading to the nearby mall. I stood at the corner by the street she would take to reach me and waved her in. The white Escalade slowed and I saw the white dog sitting up in the passenger seat. His eyes were squinting at the air-conditioning blowing his way. The woman turned onto my street, stopped, and put on her flashers.

She had attached one of her own dog's leashes to his collar I could see when she handed him over. She had brought her young daughter with her, and told me that her daughter could communicate with animals. "He loves you," the little girl said to me. That's what he told her? I thought: Why didn't he tell her where he lived and save the mother a call? But that was just me being awful. I tried to give the woman money, which she refused, so I thanked her and her daughter, and told the little girl that I wished I had her gift.

*

It is Girl Scout cookie time, and outside the grocery store there is a table set up and covered with boxes. New this year is a gluten-free option; the flavor is toffee. This is the kind I buy two boxes of, and the girl I hand the money to is the girl I gave away. Not every girl I see is the one I left behind. I have to be in a mood in order for this certainty to hijack my day. Not every girl is even the right age, but that doesn't make any difference. It's been how many years, and I see her—the girl I never saw—wherever I go. I never made a list, and don't keep count of the number of times I see her. But man, she gets around.

We have taken road trips together. I am the driver, of course, and she the imagined passenger as we cross the southern states from Florida across the Gulf coast into Louisiana. I show her New Orleans, I show *myself* New Orleans since I've been there so few times. You feel fifty percent hipper just walking down a street in that city, even if it's the wrong street. Forty dollars to park for the day—happy to pay it in New Orleans. I don't drink or party, so in New Orleans I'm a wallflower. I'm more of a one-to-one type anyway, and the girl, the imagined passenger, that's okay with her. I used to travel with men who brought guidebooks. It made a trip feel like school, having to learn about churches and trade routes, agriculture and exports. I'm not opposed to learning something, but I like a more associative experience in a new place. Especially when the new place is old. I would rather learn about a place after I have left it.

A road trip with the imagined passenger does not need a destination. We can turn back anytime we want, go to another city if we get where we were going and find out we're not interested after all. No need for souvenirs as she is not really there. But I keep the seat belt buckled over the empty seat.

*

The day before the Twin Towers fell, I attended a memorial service for one of my best friends. There were so many people there—more than four hundred—and we filled the polished private club. The next morning, watching the horror on TV, I was glad my friend had not had to see this. And immediately realized the mistake in that. He was a New Yorker, and would not have wanted to be spared the anguish. He would have rushed to offer what help he could, and been proud to stay in his neighborhood, which was only blocks away. He would have breathed in the toxic clouds that followed, in love with the injured city. His natural eloquence would have comforted others. But he was dead; he was already dead.

*

Years ago, I bought fancy onesies from a catalog for a colleague's baby. Ever since, I have received that catalog four times a year. Rather than put it in recycling, I let myself get pulled in, and follow the narrative of the tiny outfits worn by child models wearing lipstick. The catalog comes from England, and one could do worse than dress a child from its pages.

I never tracked her in terms of what she might be wearing at a certain age. I didn't think about what she might be learning, or when she learned it. I don't know the age that a child is taught long division.

Those clothes in the English catalog include dresses with gold tulle skirts and teensy cashmere sweaters. Not things one can throw in a washing machine when a baby gaks up lunch. I guess these are ceremonial clothes, and anyway there must be countless babies who have hurled on their christening gowns. Having never seen someone christened, I don't know what I'm talking about.

*

Today new signs are posted on the walkways of the botanical gardens. The first instructs visitors not to carve their initials in the bamboo. Behind the outer bark are the cells that carry water and sugar to all parts of the tree, though here many poles are already covered as high as a man can stand with names inside of hearts, threatening the hollow culms.

The second sign is smaller, and it turned up in three places: SNAKES, COTTONMOUTH NEST. The places the signs went up look no different from the rest of the spread. Like the venomous snakes won't slither over to a nonnesting area? The bromeliad gardens, for example? The signs are only inches from the walkway where women push strollers. Good luck, visitors!

*

The beach towns near here are covered with For Sale signs. Residents argue with each other over which town will be underwater first. As I have said, everyone thinks Miami, but say that to a Realtor and she will tell you that these predictions do not affect the market; sales are brisk. But the number of For Sale signs does not seem to change, as many as every other house on some Gulf coast drives. Walking along the water on a seventy-degree February day, the mildest of breezes not even rippling the water where dolphins leap in pods, and pelicans swoop down on fish, I could believe the danger was not real. But I have shown myself to be a person who does not recognize danger.

*

At a frozen yogurt place, I stood in line behind a woman holding a baby, about a year old, and dressed in a diaper. I watched as the mother carried the baby up to the flavor I planned to get, and coaxed the chubby fingers to touch the spouts where the yogurt came out, so the baby could feel the icy peaks of chocolate and vanilla left over from the last person who got some. I looked at the store attendant, like *do something*, but the attendant—a teenage girl in a uniform— smiled at the mother and the diapered baby. What the hell was wrong with them? Or what was wrong with me? No, what was wrong with *them*?

*

A friend in a long, successful marriage, her children grown, said to her husband in their house in New York's Chelsea, "I think I need to go to India and teach needy children to read." Her husband said, "I'm pretty sure you can find children to teach on Twenty-third Street." He was right. And she did. And felt better.

She told me this on a day when I was thinking about situational ethics. I was thinking about it for around two minutes, but still. As if anyone needs an even murkier situation than usual to figure out. And of course it had to do with the home, with the question of what I would have done if I had known what my decision meant at the time. Excuses abounded. But other women managed who had had a harder time. But a harder time for *them*. My hard time was still too hard for me, so the argument with myself was moot.

Tried a nap the other day. Maybe it is a thing you have to get the hang of. Nappers say they wake up refreshed. I have only felt refreshed walking into a bracing lake in Maine. Not every thought of Maine is something to do with the home.

*

In the old part of downtown, where small bungalows have not been gentrified, I have a good time with Lois, the patient who loves to talk about desire. She and I agree that if liked, we had wanted to be desired; if desired, we had wanted to be liked. Not instead, in addition. But it felt to me like wearing shoes on the wrong feet, and touching one knee to the painted white line, waiting for the gunshot to start the race.

The only race I ever ran was the midnight run in Central Park on New Year's Eve, in costume. I did it four years in a row. Close to six thousand people ran from staggered starting points while a rock band played and twenty minutes of first-rate fireworks went off. The paper cups of water on tables along the route were replaced with plastic cups of champagne. The course was only four miles long, but it was midnight and it was cold. Some of the runners added bulk in elaborate costumes and masks, but all I did—still the English teacher then—was write AND, AND, AND all over the number pinned to my shirt; I went as a run-on sentence. There was an official time clock at the finish line, and I was not the last person to cross it. Then it was off to a diner on the West Side for cheesecake at 2:00 A.M.

*

The colleague at school that I ran with got weaker each year until she walked the course the final time. She urged me to run ahead and meet her at the end. The year after that I ran the race alone. On that holiday afternoon I was stuck in traffic that made the drive two hours longer. Sitting on the southbound Hutch, not moving, I thought: She would have wanted these two hours stuck in traffic; she would have welcomed two more hours in a car, on a road, on this earth.

*

Peril, Peril, Peril, Peril—Cloudland's four little girls in white.

*

What will you do with all that extra time?—the question people ask women whose children are soon to move out. I've been asking myself that question since I left the girl at the home.

*

I learned from the next-door neighbor, an attorney for the city, about the tiny white cross with the night-light on it that you can't miss out there on the grassy median where you turn to get to my house. It commemorates a boy who was struck and killed by a car there, sixteen years ago. His family has moved away, but one of the dead boy's teachers keeps flowers blooming there. The problem, according to the city attorney, is that the dead boy's teacher planted nonindigenous species, and they spread and choked out what belongs here. I heard yelling out there, and it was a woman and my next-door neighbor who wanted to dig up her plantings. He tried to get me to cut down an invasive tree in my front yard, but since it isn't *my* yard, that ended that.

*

"You know, Jesus gave us his commandment: 'You are to love your neighbor as yourself.' You are seeing neighborliness in *action!* God bless you out of all your troubles. Twill take *time* and *dollars*, though. Your caring neighbor, (ret.) Professor Ken Warmley."

This accompanied a handwritten list titled "Your Priorities" that my neighbor who does not believe in climate change delivered. According to him, my top priority was the clearing of the easement that the utilities company had hacked to pieces. My elderly neighbor listed four services I might call to get an estimate for this job, which the owners of the house I'm renting have refused to do. He has annotated the list such that next to the first name he has written, "He's been my mow-blow-go man for years." Beside the second name listed he had written, "He's a healthy young black man." What—was I looking to buy a slave? I'm told not to take this the way it sounds, that I'm in the South, but I did not end up hiring the "healthy young black man" because he did not have a truck and thus could not haul away the butchered trees. I found a YouTube site headed "Tree Cut Fails." The man who said the utilities company does to trees what Hitler did to Jews got more comments than anyone else. "Crybaby," someone wrote. "You want electricity, don't you?" At least "Tree Cut Fails" narrows it down from all the other fails. Thank God we can't yet photograph a conscience, or a crisis of confidence, or a lapse in moral rigor, or the next thing over from regret.

*

The woman I had run the midnight race in Central Park with—she left her house to a friend in her will, and did not tell the woman that she had done so. She made out the will when she was dying an early death, forgoing the gratitude of her friend, a single mother, who would inherit the house. She did not need to be thanked. It was so clean, the way she did this. Her generosity lived on after she died.

*

On a Tuesday morning Lois—still my favorite of the folks that I look in on—Lois asks if I have time to sign a petition with her. She suffers from early Parkinson's, and is stoic. She has made me a kind of honorary daughter. I bring her a box of the Girl Scout cookies, and am happy to help. I open her computer and find the petition site she wants, and she shows me what she'd like me to sign. *Hell*, yeah—it's a petition directed at Mariah Carey; the goal is to persuade her not to have live baby elephants and tigers "perform" at her wedding to the billionaire. As though someone who would think this is the way to celebrate vows would be swayed by a hundred thousand people who see the cruelty in these plans. I sign my name anyway, and write a message in the message box "for extra impact." "Dear Mariah Carey," I write. "Please do not use baby elephants and tigers in your wedding." I click on Submit.

The moment you click on Submit, another petition pops up. It can be for something that has nothing to do with the awful thing you just said no to. Tonight the petition is about an alleged rapist who is about to be given a civic honor. I know nothing about the case, but sign it given the odds. Then sign one to stop the helicopter shooting of fenced-in wolves, a clean water petition for Michigan, and one for convincing a roadside attraction to donate its lonely elephant to a sanctuary where it can be amongst its kind. It's interesting to note the plea that I can say no to signing, and turn away from to get back to the making of my day.

All the next day I receive thanks for what I signed and submitted, not from the organizations that sent the petitions, but from individual elephants and wolves: "Thank you from Toshi," "Thank you from Eisha," and I know I have not done enough, can never do enough for them.

*

"Dear Mariah Carey." Just giving it another go. The diamond in her engagement ring weighs thirty-five carats and cost ten million dollars. What is worse is that she asked for it; she asked her fiancé for the ring that cost this much. And the next worse thing is that he bought it for her. Let's not even start to think how that much money could have kicked poverty's ass. I see that another entertainer, one more talented than she, refers to her now as Pariah.

*

In an unshaded city park I walk through sometimes, a young woman I have seen and said hello to before tells me that her divorce has finally gone through. We had never spoken about a pending divorce; I didn't know she was married. But I congratulated her, and said what a relief it must be. Yes, she said, she felt so much lighter already. This is a big deal, I said, newly sage. We wished each other well. I wondered if there were children involved. Someone else might have invited her out for a drink. But I felt I had treated her news with respect, and isn't that more than one often gets? Maybe the just-divorced woman was making a pitch for friendship. Maybe she was telling everyone she saw. Let a couple of months pass, and I won't remember this woman got divorced. I am the one to tell a secret to; I won't remember it no matter how incendiary.

*

Lois tells me that Native Americans use the yellow webs of the banana spider for fishing line. And that thirty-three percent of banana spiders are poisonous. It's a strange stat to reckon with, and I don't want to know more. In her yard, as in mine, giant dried-out banana leaves turn ashy and float about the lawn, coiled into the shape of a sawed-off plaster cast. Ghostly, and unnerving, there seems to be no end of them. No end, either, to the swordlike fronds that come crashing down from the too-tall palms. How can so many plants dry out when there is so much rain?

Lois is eager to tell me about karst. Her grandson studies geology, she says, and he wants her to spread the word. Karst goes along with frack quakes and other disasters brought on by pumping volumes of liquid into porous, rocky earth. Subterranean geology is a frightening field, she says, detailing the mounting incidence of karst-caused sinkholes and underwater caves, none of it good news except for the occasional supernatural beauty of cenotes that fill with the clearest water in beachy places like Tulum, in Mexico. What some of us in this state have to look forward to is not floating on our sun-bronzed backs in cenotes but our houses falling ninety feet into a suburban sinkhole with no time to do anything about it.

She says that karst is what's left from the dissolution of limestone and other soluble rock, the rock that can layer over itself, its air pockets accruing to gather water that is forced into it in the search for oil and gas. That last I read on the Internet. The quakes this practice causes are growing in both size and frequency, Lois says, and scientists—including her grandson—have a saying: "Earthquakes don't kill people; buildings kill people." I appreciate that kind of specificity.

An overturned egg carton is what quadrilateral karst looks like. The area in which karst quakes, like the one in Prague, Oklahoma, occur is spreading. Houses were destroyed where never before had such a thing been a threat. Now there are glaciokarst, thermokarst, cockpit karst, and parts of the central United States that hosted only tornadoes can feel movement underground.

Sink or swim, sinkholes or springs—the Blue Springs of High Springs, Florida, and the nearby Rainbow Springs, these are gifts from God. They stay at seventy-two degrees year-round, which is too cold, the locals say, for *most* gators to occupy. Even the giant turtles can turn out to be snappers, so maybe the Caribbean-colored springs are a test: are you the kind of person who can surrender to beauty or the kind who asks her braver friends to send her photos of their swim taken with underwater cameras?

Before I leave, Lois shows me photos of TTD sessions—Trash the Dress—in which underwater weddings in Mexico's Riviera Maya cenotes are photographed. The cautionary note from the photographer who posts his floaty photos: "A wet wedding dress becomes heavy."

Recently I watched a teenage couple swim. The young woman lowered herself into the clear blue springs and swam to the nearby mouth of the river where the water turns tannic—the word she used—from the decomposition of leaves. I walked along on the dirt trail alongside the springs. There is an actual line of demarcation between the benign, inviting springs and the suddenly opaque brown water in which it is impossible to see what is beside you.

*

There are stories about women who were found to be carrying a calcified fetus for upward of thirty years. The women had no idea this was the case. In the stories I heard, the women said they experienced no symptoms. Would they retrace their health for all of those years, newly able to attribute a mysterious lethargy or unexplained heaviness of spirit, a hesitation in the face of adventure? The point at which the fetus stopped growing would of course be a factor. What to do with the knowledge that your body turned against what was growing, rendered it a tumor, to use a term close to what it was.

The correct term is "lithopedion." It means "stone baby." Women can have a stone baby and still give birth to a healthy child. A woman in China was found to have the longest known case: for sixty-five years she had carried the calcified fetus. Second longest is believed to be the woman in Chile who, at ninety-one, found out she had carried one for more than sixty years when she got an X-ray after a fall. She said she could feel a lump on her stomach, and it reminded her of her husband and their unfulfilled dream of having a child. Apparently not every woman with the condition can have a child. On slow news days you can watch a feature on women like this. Of the documented cases, only a small percentage of the women chose to have the stone baby removed.

*

There must be a word for the state of going about your business without knowing something key, and with someone else knowing it, and knowing too that there could come a time when you *will* know it. I think the name of this state is The Way We Live Now, or The Way Things Have Always Been, or the oldest narrative there is: Things Are Not as They Seem.

Things were not as they seemed at the home, of course. Yet despite having read the journalist's book, I am not searching for the girl. If she is even alive, she would not be the girl I have lived with all these years. What does that make me, not posting her birthday on the website for the book?

*

I thought the woman in the waiting room called her son Tie-Dye. But when he jumped out of his chair and knocked into another waiting patient, she scolded him in the old-fashioned way, using his full first and middle names: "Tyler Dylan!" I had driven the ninety-year-old former CEO to the doctor when his grandson was unable to at the last minute. He asked me how much debt I thought his young doctor carried. He said you can't graduate doctors who owe $300,000 in loans and put them to work for socialized medicine salaries. My neighbor across the street does not believe in going to doctors, he told me, even after I saw him getting his mail with a large bandage covering much of the back of his head. At this rate he might need to hire me, though I have never told him what I do. He has simply never asked, though he did ask if I would like to shower at his house when I mentioned the nonworking drains in mine.

Two things broke today in the cursed house. I say "curs-ed," using two syllables. A man I once thought I liked struggled to say something ugly at the end, and what he came up with was calling me "the curs-ed seed from the curs-ed tree." I like parting shots; you can't take them seriously and they're often pretty funny.

The things that broke today were the ceiling—a substantial leak—and the central air-conditioning unit, which I had asked the owners to replace when I learned how old it was, to which the owners rightly said, "It's working *now*." And in a dozen places on the roof, ferns are growing from the inside out, spreading in what looks like time-lapse photography.

If everything could stop growing for a while! That's what I wanted all those years ago when I didn't yet know what to do with what was growing in me, and was trying to ride out recklessness and passion, rebellion and decisions based on what I knew at the time. And the question I still field is the one I still can't answer: Could I have known what was happening at the home? Was there a way I could have found out? First, I would have had to have suspicions. But I was—we all were—self-absorbed. We wanted out, and we believed what we were told that would expedite our departures. None of us had the money that, we were told, would guarantee the babies would go to good homes. But we would find out how to get it! We agreed to this condition of our care and the care of what started out as ours, and I was not the only one who managed to meet the terms. When one is halfway presentable and young, there are many menial jobs waiting, and if you are a woman of her word, you can do what you signed on to do. As I do now with those in my quasi-professional care.

For months until the place was rebuilt, the home was char on the land. Nothing left but the adjacent apple orchard, far enough from the flames. A random camper told me about it; he had witnessed the fire, and thought to tell me about it as simply something he had seen, having no knowledge of the place in relation to me.

The fire—when I read what went on at the home, I thought the fire was purification, at least as much as destruction. Burn out the history, and burn out the proof. Burn hotter, and burn out the ghosts.

*

In scorching sun, I opened the door to my car and saw that the front seats were covered in swarms of ants. They had colonized the car, having found a French fry between the seats and dragged it up and over the console so that it was in the driver's seat; salt trailed across the upholstery. I remembered a tip from a local, that should you find a swarm of ants, put down a trail of coffee grounds instead of spraying them with repellent. But I had gone to my car to drive to *get* coffee; there was none in the house. It was far from the worst thing to have happened in this place, but I didn't think I'd have to face an infestation in the car.

"Oh, that shouldn't happen," said the climate change–denying neighbor from across the street. I had barely looked up from squashing the ants with napkins I'd found in the back, as yet unswarmed, seat, when there he was, and at ninety or eighty-eight years of age, how had he crossed our two yards and the street so fast?

"But it did happen," I countered.

"Only in the last couple of years," he maintained. He felt himself to be the neighborhood historian, and under the guise of Christian neighborliness, turned up more and more often with corny jokes. Recently he had distributed a self-published ring-bindered book that he had printed by hand in looping pencil. He had titled this gift *A Patriarch Remembers Some of His Neighbors.* Glancing through later, I would see that he blamed an ancient run of Peeping Toms down the block on the fact that the boys' mothers "worked outside the home." I skipped ahead to the last page, where I saw my name underlined as a new member of the neighborhood whom he had not yet gotten to know "well enough."

"You look like you could use a humor break," he said.

I was in for it. One could not avoid what was coming—a lame joke about a long-married Norwegian couple. Why Norwegian? Because he subscribed to a sort of Norwegian joke compilation. Maybe he was Norwegian. I kept my eyes on the ants in my car till the joke had crawled to its end. He said that I should feel free to come over anytime I wanted to hear another—"that is, if you can still hear," he added, chuckling. Thinking, no doubt, that I too was infirm. Maybe that was what ants in your car signaled—a level of infirmity that itself was no joke, but that opened the gates for a cornball neighbor to welcome you into his decline. In his self-published, hand-printed book, the self-anointed patriarch remembered the attorney and his wife next door as people of "international kindness" who had hearts large enough to take in four homeless girls.

*

How long can one hold oneself away from those one loves most? The reasons can be persuasive, but what about the one who matters most, yet is findable neither here nor there? Wouldn't that suggest that one place is as good as another?

When I think of her, I remember that part of the appeal of swimming in warm water is the amniotic quality when you float. I like to float facedown and pick twigs like toothpicks from the filters in the pool. You want to be careful if you go to clean a screen; tiny toads get trapped there along with palm meadows, the nicer way to say palmettos. When the clouds start to rumble, I leave the pool I was not supposed to swim in for two more days due to the extra chlorine added to knock out the thickening sludge.

*

Tornado alleys are getting bigger every year. It's another result of "the controversy." There is something to learn from the stunned people who see everything they own destroyed in minutes, and who build again on the same spot once heavy equipment has cleared the wreckage. What are these people made of? Courage and faith will take you so far. Is it a kind of nobility? I know they love the land, and it is home, and they don't feel the land betrayed them, or God.

The local weather channel broadcasts the number of lightning strikes each hour in a storm. If this house is struck and I survive, you won't see the owners hire a contractor to set reconstruction in motion. "Sustainability" is a word not often used anymore in the geological sciences, not in this part of the country. Instead, the word "resiliency" shows up, maybe the word "adaptation."

Thanks to Lois pointing me in the direction of her interests, I learn about the Salton Sea in California. The dried-out seabed is home to geothermal plants that are daily increasing the number of earthquakes to a "swarm," there on the southern end of the San Andreas Fault, which will likely travel north to wipe out Los Angeles. Those who work there know that what they do is a grave threat and that damage and loss of life would be extreme, but they keep on doing what threatens so many while geologists point to the bubbling mud in the ground beside the plant, a place where pressure is both aggravated and relieved. This little circle of bubbling mud will make no difference to whatever is ahead that we will bring upon ourselves.

*

I have not spoken of Mr. Davis in a while. He is a row to hoe. The flirting is nearly constant, though he has not tried to give me diamonds, nor does he tell Norwegian jokes. Things go best with him when I can interest him in TV. We have begun to watch the true-crime shows in which people who do away with each other make stupid mistakes that get them caught: A disgruntled man in the Midwest delivers pipe bombs done up as packages to his rival business partners, killing them both. Then he sets himself up as the third bombing victim to remove himself from suspicion. But the package he said he found in his car's driver's seat, the one that exploded and injured him, was determined by forensics to have exploded in the passenger's seat. Only because he called attention to himself was he discovered to have murdered his rivals.

*

And now a horror next door. The neighbor, the city attorney in his fifties, has been arrested for sexual abuse of two of his four adopted daughters. The mother was out of town when the news broke. Seven unmarked cars were parked in front of their house and in front of mine. The cars were there for most of the day, and it was not until the fifth hour that I saw two officers standing outside, wearing plain clothes and badges. They said they could tell me nothing more than that a police investigation was under way, and that I was not in danger. I had to wait until the next morning's newspaper came out to learn the ugly news.

Within days, he was released on bail and put under house arrest. I saw nothing except the garbage containers at the end of their drive on Wednesday night for pickup on Thursday morning. There were a couple of lights on in the house, but the curtains were closed. The mother of the girls was rumored to have returned. And then, a week to the day of the scandal breaking, the man next door drove to a local fishing camp and rented a canoe. He paddled out onto the gator-inhabited lake, and stayed on the lake all night through a storm. In the morning, he paddled toward the shore, presumably to return the canoe, but when he saw the police waiting, he pulled out a gun and killed himself.

Those of us who would like to help the girls don't know where they were taken. Of course the police cannot reveal their safe location. Their job is to protect those girls, as their parents did not.

*

Shocking the pool did nothing to clear the new red algae, and now the pool is also leaking. No telling where the water is going, but if it floods the nearby Presbyterian church, I'm sure the congregation will let me know. Overnight, even in rain, banana spiders craft a strand of strong web across the front door at the level of my sunburned face.

*

I told my old friend Julia that Tropical Storm Julia had just slammed into the Georgia coast. She said, "We'll have to watch me closely as I seem to be gathering strength."

*

What I don't have anymore: a sense of direction, an interest in art, a New York license plate.

What I need: board shorts, rash guard, flip-flops, SPF, battery-powered radio, three days' worth of water.

A difference here: The Village, singular, is an assisted-living community. The Villages, plural, is a plush retirement community a couple of hours south. The Villages mails brochures to people fifty-five and older. There is no targeting of "seniors" for The Village that I am aware of. Several of my patients live in an assisted-living facility that is not as nice as The Village, singular, but is still a pleasant place with heated pool.

*

In the market, I ask the clerk for jicama, then pronounce it two other ways before he knows what I want. There is tangerine juice on ice for one month a year, but which month is that, I keep meaning to ask.

*

In the morning, an inversion layer, and a note from Julia: "I'm just headin' off the coast aimlessly. I haven't had much impact. Nothing but depression. Tropical, but nonetheless, depression. Headin' out to sea. Good-bye, Georgia, good-bye, Carolina."

*

Armadillos seen dead in the road since my arrival: twenty-nine. Night-blooming cactus I've seen flower on the one day a year that they flower: one. But it still was luck.

A month before the scandal involving the attorney next door, I saw him pulling weeds out of the forested line between our houses. I was driving by when I saw this odd sight, odd because he was on my side of the property line, and by the time I had circled back he was gone. I found out a couple of days later when I interrupted his run that he had been pulling not weeds but an invasive species of plant that, he said, was poised to take over the landscape if we didn't do something about it. But it's pretty, is what I said. I had cut sprigs with the small purple berries to place in a short crystal vase. This was the way I learned that he cared for the local ecology or, put another way, he was practicing despoiling what was beautiful that had come from somewhere else to take up residence on his turf.

Those girls did not have to end up with him. One traces back the variables: had the neighbors made the trip a month later, had they not made the trip at all, had they visited an orphanage in this country instead. We in the neighborhood still want to do something for the girls, wherever they are.

The employees at the home assured us that our babies would be raised in good families. They needed nothing more than our permission to be taken in by these kind people.

*

Driving with the gospel station on, the one that comes in or not depending on the weather, when—happiness. Tasha Cobbs is singing, "There's a miracle in this room with my name on it . . ." She incites her audience to joy with her song "Put a Praise on It." She is a powerhouse, a minister all can follow, making the case that anyone can be healed.

*

In what must have been one of the owners' boys' rooms before I moved in, I peeled rocket ships off the walls. Before I touched them and realized they *could* be peeled off, I had thought I would have to spackle over the gouges in the wall I would make. I had not bothered to get permission from the owners of the house. The plasticine decals came up without pulling off the paint beneath.

In the little girl's room down the hall, there is a decal of a tree, and it's going to remain on the wall. I thought it was a dogwood at first, but I looked in a book of trees and it is, in fact, the tree of life. I felt chastened, and would rather it had been a dogwood. But there is no arguing with what I now see should be capitalized, the Tree of Life.

*

On the whiteboard at the wetlands preserve has been added under "Sightings"—"one park ranger." She is patient and kind, so I'm glad to see her acknowledged. She will help people who can't walk get into her dune buggy and then drive them along the pebbled paths that a wheelchair can't manage so that those who can't get around on their own can still see every part of the park. Shovelers have been sighted, according to the board, as well as four cottonmouths. Can't these strike from the plantings along the paths? Unlikely, the park ranger says—they prefer to be closer to the water, she says instead of saying no.

*

When a guy in a pickup drives up and offers to blow the leaves off my roof for a very low price, I ask him if he is insured, knowing he will lie. I tell him to go ahead, but before he positions the ladder he says he did some work at the house next door the day before, and the woman there offered him all of her husband's clothes. She offered him his shoes too, he said, but the shoes were the wrong size. He did not know why she had offered to give him her husband's clothes, and in telling him, I have become a gossip.

His is not the only truck I have seen parked next door. A carpet cleaner spent a day out front, as did an air-conditioning installation van and a yard maintenance truck and trailer from the company Lawn and Order. What I'm watching for is a For Sale sign in the yard.

Many years ago I went to a friend's fiftieth birthday party. She lived in the Midwest—it had been forever since I'd seen her—and her mother threw the party in the house my friend had grown up in. All those years later, her mother was selling the house, but she took it off the market that week so everyone would have a place to stay. I could see the holes the stakes had made where For Sale signs had been replaced: banners with my friend's name flew there instead for days.

There was a guest wearing a mannish canvas coat; she suggested we walk up the nearby hill to a burned-out estate. There is a kind of weary peace that comes with getting to a place long after others have discovered it. Even someone's burned-down house, the stone footprint grown over with ivy and trumpet vine. It was a party I was glad to have traveled to. When I left the house after midnight, I felt like I had been home.

*

It would be nice to have raspberry canes in a backyard; a girl could learn to pick the berries without getting poked. A father or mother could show a young girl how to do this.

In Maine, the artist's wife would sometimes sunbathe on their dock in a white bathing suit, then leave the still-dry suit hanging from a hook on the pier. Her husband said he liked to see this—the dry white bathing suit moving in a breeze, his wife having gone inside to read.

*

The wedding is off, and I will not have to write Mariah Carey anymore.

*

Next week I am going to see another psychic. This person lives down the block from Lois, so I can go right over on Tuesday morning. After I see the psychic, Lois wants me to give her a recap over tea.

The psychic is likely to tell me that I will fall in love. This is what everyone thinks one wants to hear. But I don't want to fall in love in the sense that a psychic might mean it. I don't want a romance, if that is what she predicts. But love—sure, keep it coming. In another form. Not a man and not a woman. An animal, a place, or a cause. I would like to fall in love again with any and all of these.

So many people need help right now, and one doesn't need to be in love to give it. Helping *is* love; that is what it can look like. That is one way you know when love is near. No psychic needed for this. Still, I am going to pay the psychic to tell me what she wants me to know. Then I will have a cup of tea with Lois, and entertaining her is a good enough reason for me to see it through.

*

I remember being surprised to learn that asking for help is a sign of strength. Someone who knew what she was talking about set out to convince me of this when I told her I had failed to gauge the point at which I had to stop asking for help, had to figure something out for myself. Why was it hard to see this as strength? I'd seen people all my life who felt it was a matter of character to puzzle through a problem by themselves. Self-sufficiency as a point of honor—I was persuaded by this. But help could come in so many forms.

Help came in the form of water over and over. Hot water in a cup of tea, warm water in a pool with no one else wanting to use it, surf covering your feet at an ocean beach when the tourists had left and you no longer needed to buy a day pass.

The day before the appointment with the psychic, the storm we were warned of hit hard. Just before midnight, I heard a tremendous crack, and the power went out. Nothing to do till morning, when I called the fire department to put out the smoking tree that had cracked open near the ground, an enormous oak that fell onto power lines and spewed smoke from its hollowed core. A burning tree, and then the psychic who, it turned out, spoke of past lives, notably the one that ended when I died in the London Fire of 1666. She said I was forced to jump from a burning building, a body falling from the sky—we did not have to say aloud what that image conjured. She said I did not need to be afraid of flying because the thing I feared had already happened. I had not told her that I was afraid to fly.

At Lois's house after, we ate salted grape tomatoes and I told her about the visit. The following week, I brought each of us a marbled black and white notebook; the psychic had suggested writing down what our younger selves wanted to say. How much younger? The psychic had suggested four years old. But I didn't know any four-year-olds, didn't know what they had to say. Humoring Lois, I pretended to "hear" my four-year-old self, but the voice I tried to hear was the voice of the girl in the apple tree, a girl who had grown into an apple tree in the orchard at the home. That girl, she asked how it was that nobody saw them. I took her literally—I pictured these babies buried in the orchard becoming part of the roots of the trees. "And the children in the apple-tree/ Not known, because not looked for."

*

"Five ducks provide eggs to feed a family for years." Five ducks cost fifty dollars. This from the World Vision catalog that showed up in my mail. "A goat and two chickens supply a steady supply of protein to feed children and transform futures." A goat and two chickens cost $110. A dairy cow: "One cow can give up to 5,000 gallons—or 80,000 glasses—of milk in its lifetime." One dairy cow costs $700. Education for girls has three choices: $150, $75, and $40. "Studies show that when a woman has an education, her whole community benefits."

I will bring the catalog along to show the CEO. He can afford it all.

*

Driving past a general store in a rural county, I come upon a Hispanic kid hoisting an old boom box, a Keith Richards guitar solo blasting, the kid yelling, *"Keef! Keef!"* A brush with greatness.

*

The home allowed us the illusion for a while that we had done the right thing. A selfless choice, which might come to be a comfort when we questioned ourselves later, when our strength had returned, and the milk had dried up, and maybe we had found jobs and not-bad places to live. Maybe we would tell everyone we got to know about it, and maybe we would never tell anyone ever. What would we look for in a person we might tell? Did we override a sense of unease because the home was the only place that welcomed us? And wasn't it pleasant to walk along mown paths through tall grass? And when we left, we found an apple wrapped in a napkin for the trip had been placed inside our totes.

But the employees who suddenly quit, the fire, the ruinous truth.

The journalist, the author of the book, born there.

*

I watched a true-crime show with difficult Mr. Davis about a murder: A woman's body was found in an orchard. Her husband had killed her, and tried to make it look as though his wife's horse had thrown her. He said she must have been killed when her head struck a rock where she landed. But detectives noticed that the rock was the only one in the orchard. They did not accept the theory that the dead woman's husband put forward.

The only dumber thing the husband might have done would be to have placed the side of the rock with which he had bashed in his wife's skull, the side covered with blood, face*down* beneath her head. He had wanted the money from her life insurance policy. He wanted to spend it on someone else, but he would spend the rest of his life in prison.

Before the detectives failed to find a single other rock, did the man feel apprehension or anticipation? Were his thoughts about the future fueled by fear, or did the urgency come from the courage to act, to do anything required to be with the one he loved? Stendhal wrote, "If it were necessary to commit a murder that I might see you, I would become a murderer."

*

Macouns had been my favorites, but you couldn't always get them in stores. Or you thought you were buying them when really you were buying McIntosh, mislabeled. The flesh of Macouns is not as soft. The Macoun has a taste of berry to it; it has a short growing season, and a high susceptibility to powdery mildew and cedar apple rust. Neither kind is as good for you as a green Granny Smith.

I only trust an apple I can pick from a tree, but since reading the reporter's book, I won't be doing that again.

Though if I were to visit the orchard at the home, I'll bet I could find a single rock to rest my head against.

Acknowledgments

With great thanks to my editor, Nan Graham, for her close attention, galvanizing suggestions, and unerring wisdom; to Susan Moldow, for her valuable support; and to my agent Liz Darhansoff, for her good judgment and longtime friendship. My thanks to Tamar McCollom, Kara Watson, and everyone else at Scribner who had a hand in bringing out this book.

For various kinds of help with the creation of these stories, I want to thank Jill Ciment, Martha Gallahue, Allan Gurganus, Chiu-yin Hempel, my brothers Gardiner and Peter Hempel, Bret Anthony Johnston, Pearson Marx, Jill McCorkle, Rick Moody, Laurel Nakadate, Paola Peroni, Roger and Ginny Rosenblatt, Julia Slavin, Pat Towers, and Lou Ann Walker. Thank you, Syd Straw, for the very thing that allowed me to finish "The Chicane" thirty years after I started it.

I thank my fellow members of Compassion Care, who remain inspirations to me as they work to save the lives of dogs in extremis, in particular: Rebecca Ascher-Walsh,

Acknowledgments

Jeff Latzer, Yolanda Crous, Laurie Daniels, Carol Roth-schild, and Dr. Evelyne Cumps.

And I thank the always generous Chuck Palahniuk for telling me about the Butterbox Babies and Bette Cahill's book about the little-known, horrific crimes in Nova Scotia. His research had shown him that he could not write about this because "there's nothing funny about it." So he offered it to me in case I could make something of it. This gift was the beginning of "Cloudland," which takes its title from the haunting painting by Gloria Vanderbilt.

Notes

3 "not even the rain has such small hands" by E. E. Cummings from "somewhere I have never travelled, gladly beyond."

21 "blue reef-scarred sea" is from Joseph Conrad, in *The Shadow Line: A Confession*, part 1.

23 The doll tornado is an installation titled *Toynado* at Elsewhere, the art museum/thrift store in Greensboro, North Carolina. The creator of the piece is Kim Holleman.

79 The painting is *Shock and Awe 20* by Arnold Mesches.

81 *Cloudland* is a painting by Gloria Vanderbilt. The story "Cloudland" owes a significant debt to the nonfiction book *Butterbox Babies: Baby Sales, Baby Deaths, the Scandalous Story of the Ideal Maternity Home*, by the Canadian journalist Bette Cahill. She published the horrifying and complex true story in 1992 and, with new revelations, in 2007.

95 *Water Damage* is a painting by William Wegman.

Stories Previously Published

"Sing to It": *O, The Oprah Magazine*

"The Orphan Lamb": *Harper's, Life Is Short—Art Is Shorter, The Best American Nonrequired Reading 2011*

"A Full-Service Shelter": *Tin House, The Pushcart Prize XXXVIII* (2014)

"The Doll Tornado": *Subtropics*

"I Stay with Syd": *Tin House,* tenth anniversary issue

"The Chicane": *Washington Square Review, The Best American Short Stories 2017*

"Greed": *Ploughshares,* guest-edited by Elizabeth Strout

"Fort Bedd": *Subtropics*

"Four Calls in the Last Half Hour": *Harvard Review*

"The Correct Grip": *O, The Oprah Magazine*

"The Second Seating": *The Harvard Advocate*

"Moonbow": *The American Scholar*

"Equivalent": *The Southampton Review*